Presents of the Undead

My Life Among the Undead:

Book 11

Camara M. Bragdon

My Life Among the Undead **Books**

By

Camara M. Bragdon

Friend of the Undead

Yard Sale of the Undead

Secrets of the Undead

Carnival of the Undead

Holiday of the Undead

Reunion of the Undead

Election of the Undead

Legacy of the Undead

Quests of the Undead

Rescue of the Undead

DEDICATION

This book is dedicated in memory of Eve Biner, a library volunteer and honorary staff member. A former librarian herself, this wonderful woman was a true friend of the library both in deed and word. She gave so much of her time to help improve the needs of the library.

CHAPTERS

Chapter One:
Yes, Shelly, There is a Santa Claus

Being the ruler of a thousand islands during the Christmas season is not as busy as one would think. I thought that being the vampire queen of Peregrin would involve more holiday parties. Instead, I sat on the bleachers in the underground room of Castle Delorean and watched my husband train with various members of the castle's staff. I wasn't dressed for a sporting event in my purple blouse, black dress pants, and black flats.

Sitting next to me was my father, Timothy Anderson, in his crisp, white chef's jacket. He glanced at the timer on my smartphone clock as Metallica's song, "Don't Tread on Me" echoed throughout the training room. "Shelly," he asked me, "are you really timing how long Dusty stays in the ring?"

The timer read just over two minutes. "He's doing better

than last time. Eddie said he made it a minute into the song last time."

In the ring, two men in their twenties in sleeveless shirts and shorts fought with deadly weapons One was a vampire with black curly hair and dashing green eyes. He raised a six-foot-long golden war scythe with a deadly two-foot-long blade housed in a protective covering and swung it at his opponent.

The other man quickly raised a double-bladed battle axe with similar blade protections and blocked the scythe's swing with the two-foot-long, multi-colored nylon handle. Beads of sweat dripped down from his dirty blonde short hair. He swung his weapon back at the vampire, but the ax head caught on the underside of the scythe's blade.

The vampire effortlessly yanked the ax out of the man's hand and caught it with his free hand. He safely tossed the ax aside. He then swung the six-foot-long handle at the man's legs, knocking his opponent on the mat. My husband looked over at me. "How long did he stay on his feet this time, Shell?"

"'Almost two minutes!" I said.

Eddie Van Helsing dropped both weapons and reached

out his hand to Dusty Wiliams. "You didn't break anything, did you, Dusty?"

"Nope," Dusty Williams said as he pulled himself up. The lean man towered over my husband by a few inches. "That wasn't too intense."

"Athena, pause music," Eddie said to the AI virtual assistant. Once the music had paused, he gave Dusty the battle ax back. " Are you sure you don't want one with a longer handle?"

Dusty spun the ax with both hands. "Nah, it's a great weapon."

Eddie pointed to the metal bracelet on the man's wrist. "Remember to use your shield as a weapon as well. Always be on guard."

Dusty nodded. He walked back to the bleachers and took a sip from his water bottle. "You don't have to time my failures, Shelly-your Majesty." Dusty had known me since I was a thirteen-year-old kid in another reality, and he was still getting used to the fact that I was now a powerful vampire queen.

"You're not the only one that I time their failures, Dusty. I do it for everyone. Bruce only made it fifteen seconds into his song while Andrew made it thirty seconds. And Dad--"

My father ran his finger through his short brown hair as he got up from his seat. "I can beat him," he said. He climbed into the ring. "I'm ready, Eddie," he told the vampire leaning against a corner of the ring.

"Are you sure, Timothy?" Eddie asked as he got into a fighting stance with both his war scythe and shield ready for combat.

Using his magical stretching ability, my father retrieved from across the room a curved wooden club with a metal ball attached at its end. "I'm more than ready."

Eddie instructed Athena to play the song, "Do You Hear the People Sing" from the musical Les Miserables. Even though my father is a fit, third-degree black belt, he was no match for the vampire. He only lasted five seconds. Eddie leaped up in the air and kicked the club out of my father's hand in mid-air before knocking him to the ground with the butt of the war scythe. "One day, you'll beat me, Timothy," he said as he helped my father to his feet.

"It would help if you weren't a vampire," Dad told him.

He limped out of the ring and sat back down next to me. "Your husband's confidence is getting annoying," he said.

I smiled. "Don't worry, Dad."

Eddie leaned against the ring's ropes. "Ready for another round, Dusty?"

Dusty shook his head. "No, thanks. I prefer not to have any bones broken the weekend I move in with Gunther."

Eddie shrugged. "Fine with me. Timothy?"

Dad crossed his arms over his chest and shook his head. "I don't think the queen would like it if the royal cook is injured. Anyway, I have to get back to the kitchen." My father waved goodbye to us and took the elevator upstairs.

Eddie shrugged. "I guess training's over."

I shot my hand up enthusiastically. "I want to train! I want to train!"

Eddie began to back up in the ring as a slightly terrified look appeared in his green eyes. "I've made a terrible mistake!"

I drew my magical sword from its red leather sheath on my back as I leaped off the bleachers. I landed in a graceful crouch in the center of the ring. "Athena, play 'No More Mister Nice Guy' by Alice Cooper," I instructed the AI with a smile. I pressed the underside button of the metal bracelet I always wore on my left hand and out popped the indestructible metal shield, Truth. I swung the sword I affectionately call Knowledge at my husband. "You're going down, hon," I said.

"Come on, Shelly! It's Christmas," Eddie said as he started to spin the war scythe in front of him. "Are you going to let me win this time?"

"Maybe next year," I said with a grin. I wielded Knowledge, and it clanged against the war scythe's blade.

Eddie glanced up at the entrance. "Hey, our private secretary's here. Maybe we should stop because he probably has something important to tell us."

I didn't even look at the satyr taking a seat next to Dusty. "Hey, Gunther! Is there something you need to tell us?"

The half-man, half-goat stopped talking to Dusty. "Oh, no, your Majesty. What I have to tell you and the king can wait," he said.

"Good," I replied as I ducked to avoid the war scythe. I hit

Eddie's shield with mine, shoving him to the other side of the ring. "Now I can fully concentrate on kicking your butt again."

"You know I'm going easy on you, Shell," Eddie replied as he tried to knock me off my feet with the war scythe's handle.

I grinned as I took a quick step back. "I can read your mind, hon. I'm going easy on you." Alice Cooper's song began to wrap up as I broke into a running jump. Just as the last line rang throughout the room, I landed on my husband's shield and knocked him on his back. "Booyah!" I said as he lay on the mat. I turned to face the men sitting on the bleachers. "And that, gentlemen, is how you defeat my husband," I said with a dramatic bow.

Eddie took my outstretched hand and pulled himself up. "I think you broke my ego."

We got off the training ring and approached the bleachers. "You normally don't come down to the training room, Gunther," I said. "What's going on?"

Gunther Hornicus took a slip of paper from the pocket of his chocolate-brown silk vest. "A Denise Bernard contacted you late last night via email. She has some urgent business to discuss with you, your Majesty." The twenty-something-year-old satyr read the note to make sure he got the name correct. "She'll be here in an hour."

"That'll give me time to shower," Eddie said.

"I probably need to shower as well," Dusty said. "Unless you want to have our lunch date right now, Gunther."

"Please shower, love," the satyr told him. Gunther and I watched as the two men headed off to the lockers. He smiled as he touched the tip of one of his two curved horns sitting atop his balding head. He wore his usual three-piece chocolate brown vest suit with a colorful tie. Instead of a solid pink, the tie was white with a Christmas tree print.

"I like the tie," I told him.

"Thank you. Dusty bought it for me last week."

"Is that his Christmas gift to you?"

"No, he's getting me some new cufflinks." He pointed to the tarnished silver square cufflinks on his left hand. "I've had these for a long time, and they're starting to fall apart."

"So what are you going to get him?"

"Some new cookware. What about you and the king?"

"I'm getting Eddie some new gear for his motorcycle, and I asked him for some new art supplies," I said as we got up from the bleachers and headed back to my office. "Excited about this weekend?"

The satyr smiled. "I am, and so is Dusty. He's been staying with me almost every night for the past two months, and it just makes more sense that he moves in with me. This will be my first Christmas with someone since Enoch's death." Gunther had lost his previous boyfriend to suicide three years before. Even though I had only known him for over a year, I had never seen him happier since he started dating Dusty. "What are you and the king's plans for Christmas?"

"Nothing too exciting. Eddie and I are going to exchange presents after he makes strawberry French toast, and then we are going over to my parents for Christmas dinner. You and Dusty should come."

"We are. Your stepmother already invited us."

"Good. You guys are like family," I told him. We got off the elevator and went to Gunther's desk. "This woman I'm supposed to meet, could you tell me more about her?"

"She didn't tell me anything, except that she has some urgent business to discuss with you," Gunther said as he sat down. He logged onto his computer and showed me the email.

The message was short, but not very informative. "May it please Your Majesty," the message read, "I have an urgent matter of utmost importance to discuss with you? I shall arrive at Castle Delorean tomorrow morning at 11 o'clock. Your humble servant, Denise Bernard."

I glanced at the sender's email address. "Interesting, this is someone's address, not a business one."

The satyr nodded. "I came across it when I was cleaning out the spam folder before I went to get you. I even tried a search for her online, but came up with nothing."

"That is a little weird."

"If you need extra security, I'm sure Dusty won't mind helping out."

"Let's show the king this and get his opinion. Personally, I wouldn't mind the extra security as a precaution."

I heard two sets of footsteps coming down the long hallway and turned around to see my husband and Gunther's boyfriend approaching the satyr's desk. "Eddie, could you take a look at this?" I asked.

Eddie had changed into a black blazer over a teal dress shirt with black dress pants and black dress shoes. The striped purple and teal tie I had gotten him for his birthday completed the ensemble. The vampire furrowed his brow in concern as he read the email. "I don't like that she's just showing up with barely any notice. She expects you to see her without any knowledge of your schedule."

"Well, it is the week before Christmas, and she could think my schedule is empty," I said.

"Unless you guys know who she is, this could turn into a major security issue," Dusty pointed out. He too had changed into a lavender button-down shirt under a dark gray sweater with black jeans and polished black wingtips.

"There's no trace of her online," Gunther said.

"Dusty's right, this could turn nasty," Eddie said. "I highly recommend that we have extra security when we meet with her."

"I'll check to make sure she doesn't have any weapons and can escort her in and out of the office," Dusty said.

"Station yourself by the door in our office," Eddie told him. "Anubis can be just outside the door where he normally stands guard. Speaking of which, where is that sphinx?"

"He's probably out in the garden, harassing Quinten," I said as I looked out the large bay window behind Gunther's desk. Sure enough, we all could see the sleek gray creature with a lion's body and huge gray feathery wings chasing after a half-eagle, half-lion, winged griffin. The first creature let out a howl from his jackal head as he swung his long, green python tail a little close to the glass window. We all took a step back. "That was too close," I said.

I open the glass door to the garden. "Anubis, stop harassing Quentin!" I shouted.

Both creatures paused in their terrorization of each other. The gray Sphinx is about the size of a Great Dane, but he bounded over to me like an overexcited puppy. "Anubis, reporting for duty, ma'am!" He said as he saluted me with one of his paws. Before I could say a word, the griffin rushed up next to him. "Quinten, reporting for duty, ma'am!" He, too, saluted me with a front talon.

I stifled an exaggerated sigh as I began to regret my early Christmas present to the enchanted griffin. He wanted to be part of the castle's security team with Anubis, but having an ex-rocker/slacker turned enchanted griffin and a teenage sphinx both working together was like having two kids guard a china shop. They do great guarding separately, but together they were not helpful at all.

I decided to be diplomatic with my next words. "I have a visitor arriving in less than an hour. Anubis, I need you to guard my office while the king and I meet with her. Quentin, you will patrol the skies, alert Dusty when she arrives, and help escort her to my office."

"Got it." The griffin and the sphinx saluted me again before they took off to perform their respective assignments. Dusty excused himself to stand guard at the main entrance as Eddie and I went into our office.

I sat behind my large cherry desk and turned on the computer to do a little research on our unexpected mystery guest. My foot tapped nervously against the hardwood floor as my search efforts came up empty. I got up and began to pace nervously behind my desk.

"Shell," the vampire king said without looking up from his computer. "You'll wear a hole in the floor if you don't stop that."

"I hate this feeling of not knowing anything about this person," I told him as I finished another round of pacing. "I feel helpless."

"I understand, but you're going to be safe. Both Dusty and I will be in the office with you, as well as Anubis and Quinten just outside. If she somehow gets past all of us, then Gunther will take her down with his automated crossbow gun."

I stopped pacing. "I know, but I don't like this feeling of uncertainty."

Eddie looked at me. "Did you have another vision?"

"No, I'm just nervous. That's all." Aside from being a human-turned-vampire, I also had psychic visions. I could see things from the past, present, and future. Sometimes the visions were good, but many times they were bad. I jumped when I heard the intercom buzzer ring on my landline. I rushed to my seat and pressed the button. "Yes?"

"Ms. Denise Bernard is here, Your Majesty," Gunther said.

"Should I send her in?"

"Yes, please."

The door opened, and Dusty escorted a short, thin elfin woman with fiery red hair and very nervous green eyes inside. We introduced ourselves. "Have a seat," I told her as I motioned to one of the two black leather chairs one sees in a doctor's waiting room.

She sat down and placed the oversized silver and gold purse on the floor next to her. She smoothed out some insignificant wrinkles from her bright green pantsuit which she wore over a red blouse. Tiny gold jingle bells chimed as they hit the silver zipper of her white ankle boots. "I'm sorry to intrude on you like this, Your Majesty," she apologized.

"Not a problem, Ms. Bernard," I said. "What can I help you with?

She glanced over at Dusty nervously. "Can this conversation be held in private?"

I glanced over at Eddie for his input who told me telepathically no. "I'm sorry, but my security guard stays."

She blew out a reluctant sigh. "As you wish. First of all,

my last name is not Bernard. That is my great-grandmother's maiden name. My actual last name is Doodleysqueaks, and I work for Santa up in Ho Hoboken as his press secretary."

My jaw dropped in surprise. "I'm sorry, but did you just say you're Santa's press secretary?"

"Yes," Ms. Doodleysqueaks replied as if she just told me that she worked at Wal-Mart. "Is that a problem?"

I glanced over at Eddie for his reaction to this news, but he was completely unfazed. Then I stole a glance at Dusty and saw a completely skeptical look in his eyes before quickly changing over to a complete poker face. Why were Dusty and I the only ones completely shocked by this? "No, not all," I lied. "Please, continue."

"The problems all started about four months ago. As you know, November and December are very busy times at the workshop. Early in September, Doris Claus disappeared, and that's when things started to change. Santa didn't even start a search and rescue team. The Sasquatch security team and the elfin toymakers are blaming each other for Mrs. Claus' disappearance. Santa is not doing anything about it. He's not doing anything at all. There have been multiple accidents at the toy factory, the gnomes have gone into hiding, and Santa has done nothing to help. Ho Hoboken needs your help, ma'am."

Wow, this woman is really delusional, I thought as I maintained a neutral demeanor. I decided to play along. "Well, Ms. Doodleysqueaks," I said, "I need to discuss this with the king and will give you my answer before five this evening. What is the best way to contact you?"

She pulled out an old-style flip phone from her purse and looked up her number before reciting to me. "Sorry," she apologized unnecessarily, "This is a brand-new phone."

"Don't worry about it," I said as I jotted down the number.

"Security will see you out."

"Thank you, Your Majesty. If you don't help Ho Hoboken, Christmas will be ruined forever!"

Overdramatic much? "Let me think about it," I told her. Once Ms. Doodleysqueaks had left the office, I turned to Eddie. "Wow! Was that crazy or what?"

Barely containing his excitement, he jumped out of his seat and ran to me. "I know, right? We have to go!"

"What?" I asked. This wasn't the reaction I expected from him. "Ms. Doodleysqueaks is clearly crazy! She believes that she is Santa's press secretary. Santa as in Santa Claus."

Eddie nodded. "What's so hard to believe about that?" He asked sincerely.

"Well, for one thing, Santa isn't real."

The vampire gasped in horror. "How can you say something like that?"

"Because I'm an adult and stopped believing in Santa Claus when I was a kid."

"Shelly, he is real."

I gave Eddie a skeptical look. "No, he's a myth."

Dusty came back into our office to report that the elf had left the building. "Is there anything else, Your Majesties?" he asked.

"Is Santa Claus real?" I asked him.

"Uh, no. I believe in the concept of Santa, not an actual person," the security guard replied.

"Have you told your boyfriend about your disbelief?" Eddie asked him.

"That topic has never come up."

The vampire shook his head as he pressed the intercom. "Gunther, could you come in here, please?"

"Yes, sire." Moments later, the satyr entered the office. "Is everything all right?" he asked.

"You're a reasonable man. Could you settle a debate for us? Is Santa Claus real?" I asked.

"Yes," Gunther answered. "Why is that a matter of debate?"

His boyfriend looked at him as if he had just admitted to being a serial killer. "You mean the concept of Santa is real, right, Gun?"

"No, Santa is a real person," the satyr insisted.

"Thank you!" Eddie said. "I can't believe my wife and your boyfriend think Santa isn't real."

"Could the reason be that Dusty and I are adults?" I said.

"I think I understand what is going on here," Gunther said. "Both the queen and Dusty are from another world in which Santa Claus is a fictional person."

Dusty and I both nodded.

"Here in this world, Santa is very real," Gunther explained.

"Uh-huh," I said, not even a little convinced by my private secretary's explanation.

Both Eddie and Gunther sighed. "Shell, if I pull up a live satellite stream of Ho Hoboken, will you believe us?" my husband asked as he sat back down at his desk.

I rolled my eyes. "Not everything you read on the internet is true, dear," I said as my inner librarian emerged.

Eddie said nothing as his fingers flew over the keyboard, typing out a memorized website. He hit the final key with an unnecessary flourish and said, "Ta-da!" as he turned the monitor to show me his findings.

On the screen was a satellite image of an outline of a small town in the shape of a Christmas tree. Every roof was covered in snow. Strings of tiny bright lights lined the streets.

"Is this real?" I asked.

"Of course, it is, Shell," Eddie answered.

I mulled it over for a few minutes as my doubt began to melt away. "I guess Santa is a real person. He must be thousands of years old."

Gunther shrugged. "Nobody knows, Your Majesty. Stories of Santa have been passed down for generations in my family."

"Same here," Eddie added. "Did you always get what you asked Santa for?"

Gunther smiled. "Of course. My favorite present was the panpipes. When I was ten, I asked Santa for these custom-made panpipes from prism bamboo. This type of bamboo is very rare as each stalk is a different color of the rainbow and will play a distinctive note. For example, the red stalks have a slightly lower pitch than the violet stalks. Even back then, they cost about five hundred dollars. My parents couldn't afford that kind of expensive Christmas gift, and Santa answered my letter for one."

"Like the ones you played for me on my birthday?" Dusty asked.

"The very same ones," Gunther answered with a grin.

"And here I thought the pipes were just simple pride pipes," Dusty said.

"I don't understand why they need my help," I said. "This seems more of an internal dispute in Ho Hoboken than an outside intervention. Why doesn't Ms. Doodleysqueaks ask the leaders of Ho Hoboken to take care of it?”

"Because Ho Hoboken is a territory of the Peregrin empire," the satyr explained.

"Santa is one of my royal subjects and needs my help? That settles it. I'm going to Ho Hoboken!”

Chapter Two:

Rockin' Around the Christmas Town

Denise Doodleysqueaks cowers in front of two lizard-like creatures. The smell of rotten flesh rises from a large, deep hole in the ground behind her. "I did it to save Christmas!" As the two beings start to converse with each other, an ever-shifting amoeba hovers over each one of them. As they speak in an unknown language, the amoeba changes colors. A few moments later, their conversations stop right as the taller of the two pushes the elf into the hole. A terrified scream escapes from her lips but is cut off when a large white worm with long spikes protruding from its head emerges from the hole. As it opens its large mouth,

I opened my eyes to see a blue fluffy face staring back at me with a hungry look in his eyes. The catnip dragon's adorable, pink-forked tongue licked the tip of my nose as he sat on my chest. How can a fourteen-pound cat-dragon hybrid feel like an elephant is sitting on top of you? I glanced over at my sleeping husband in envy. He fed the little guy at night while I had the honor of the morning feeding rituals. "All right, Alonzo," I told him as I petted his soft, blue scale-shaped fur. "I got the message," I said as I checked my phone for the time. 3:30 in the morning. At least, he wasn't meowing loudly, yet.

Alonzo flapped his little green bat-like wings as he flew down to the floor. I followed him to the kitchen as he weaved back and forth in front of me. "Are you hungry?" I asked him. "Meow once for yes. Meow twice for no."

His response was smacking my leg with his long, spiked tail. Fortunately, the soft, blue spikes were only for show. After giving him both wet and dry food, I went back to bed where

Eddie was propping himself up with one elbow.

"What are you doing up?" he asked.

I pointed to Alonzo who was peeking around the corner of

the bedroom door as my explanation.

Eddie looked at the catnip dragon. "You would never wake

up Shelly. Would you?"

Alonzo gave a loud meow before darting out of sight. I fell

back against my pillow. "Well, it wasn't entirely his fault," I

admitted.

"Shelly, how could you blame an innocent, cute animal?"

I was tempted to roll my eyes, but it was too early in the

morning for that kind of effort. "Hilarious, Eddie," I said flatly,

before telling him about my weird dream. "What do you think it

means?"

My husband shrugged. "I dunno."

"Super helpful, hon."

The next morning, Eddie and I boarded the Eggbeater, a

white, two-seater helicopter with yellow rotor blades on the top.

My husband had built the aircraft with the help of Cassius and the crew from the *Monte Carlo* airship. This was not the first thing with an engine the vampire has built. Several cars, all in the shape of fruits or vegetables, and two normal motorcycles were all built from scratch from his eight decades as a vampire. This was his first flying machine. We had a rule: if he built something, I could name it.

We stored our suitcase and weapons' backpack behind us. A mini cooler with my six-pack of bottled fruit dragon blood sat between the two pilots' seats. As a vampire, I only drink animal blood. Drinking human blood is highly unethical. I placed the copilot's helmet and adjusted the microphone. I wasn't a pilot by any stretch of the imagination, but I wasn't going to sit in the luggage compartment for a two-hour flight.

Eddie hopped in the pilot's seat and placed the helmet on his head. "Shelly, can you hear me?" he asked into his headset.

"Loud and clear, Eddie," I replied as I put on my seat harness. I yawned. The combination of the bizarre dream and getting up at 3 A.M. to feed Alonzo left me exhausted.

"Let's fly this thing," the vampire said as he flipped on an overhead switch. Within moments, the engine was primed and the rotors began to spin. Eddie opened the throttle completely and slowly pulled up the collective lever as he simultaneously worked the foot pedals. Soon, we were up in the air and on our way to Ho Hoboken on top of Mt. Swizzler.

Eddie landed the helicopter with ease two uneventful hours later on the large snow-covered parking lot of the Holly Jolly Inn right on the edge of Ho Hoboken. The quiet rotary blades spun to a slow stop, and we deboarded.

"Holy crap! It's freezing here!" I said as I pulled my green wool hat over my ears from the harsh winter wind. I stuffed my cold, gloved hands into the sleeves of my purple wool peacoat. "I should've brought a parka instead."

"It's not that cold," Eddie said as he grabbed our bags from the helicopter. His blue wool peacoat was only buttoned halfway. He wasn't even wearing a hat.

I stomped my supposed winter boots in the snow. "Let's get to the hotel before I freeze my butt off," I said as I removed my hands from my sleeves, took the backpack from my husband,

and put it on. Then I practically sprinted through the inn's snowy parking lot with my husband trailing behind me.

When I stepped inside the quaint, two-story inn, the pinecone smell hit me like a ton of bricks. I tried to hack politely as I navigated around the two giant Christmas trees decorated with equally giant multi-colored lights and string tinsel that thankfully became unpopular after the eighties. Several wreaths overloaded with gigantic bows hung on the red and green striped walls.

"Wow!" Eddie whispered when he arrived. "I haven't seen decorations like this since I was a kid eighty years ago."
"I think the child-sized plastic candy canes hanging from every conceivable branch really tie the place together," I whispered back. "I really hope they have a gift shop."

An elf wearing a Santa's helper outfit sat at the desk. Her reindeer-shaped name tag read "Carol." The little bell on her red and green stocking cap gave a little jingle as she saw us."Welcome to the Holly Jolly Inn," Carol said as she plastered on a huge smile.

"I'm Shelly Van Helsing, and my husband and I reserved a

room here," I said.

"Okay," she said, "May I see some identification?"

"Of course," I said as I started to reach into my purse for my wallet.

The wall warbled behind her and a cervitaur suddenly sprang through and stood next to the elf. From the waist up, he was mostly human except for his large, brown deer-like ears that flanked the large pair of velvety antlers poking through his slicked-back dark brown hair. He wore black dress pants over his two deer-shaped legs. "Mrs. Ribbonhauser, do you know who this is?" he asked in a sugary, sweet tone as he touched the bell-shaped pin on his black pinstripe suit coat. I caught a faint whiff of rotten fruit emanating from him. Was that his cologne or a basket of rotten fruit?

The woman shook her head fearfully. "No, Mr. Lander, it's the inn's policy--"

"Mrs. Ribbonhauser, this is our queen, and you are to treat her as such!"

"But--," Carol stammered. She managed to hide her gag reflex as the guy stood next to her.

The cervitaur's dark eyes narrowed at her. "Would you like a visit to the sworm?" he asked cruelly as he leaned closer to her. A terrified, sickly look appeared in the woman's eyes as she vehemently shook her head.

"Why don't you work in the gift shop while I take care of our esteemed guests?" he ordered her.
The elf let out a defeated sigh and scurried away from the desk. The cervitaur turned to us. "I apologize for her behavior, Your Majesties! My name is Claude Lander. How was your trip here?"

What was he talking about? She was doing her job, and neither Eddie nor I had asked for special favors. "No need for apologies. Ms. Ribbonhauser was very courteous to us," I told him as he blatantly ignored me and handed me our room keys.

"All right, Your Majesty. You don't need to pay for a thing. You're in Room Six. We have a gift shop for all your needs, free wifi, and continental breakfast from 6 am to 9am." He slithered out from behind the desk and attempted to take our suitcase from Eddie. "Allow me to show you to your room," He insisted as he tried to grab our luggage.

My husband yanked the suitcase out of his reach and his

cologne. "Oh, no, thank you, Mr. Lander. We can manage."

"Please, call me Claude. Mr. Lander was my prefixathixer-I mean father." The cervitaur tried again to swipe it, but Eddie quickly stepped back. "Oh, I insist!" he said. "You must be very hungry from your trip. Why don't I take your luggage to your room and unpack it while you two go have lunch at O'Tannenbaum's, the town pub?"

"Uh, we're good!" I said, still trying to understand how a non-magical person could walk through a wall. Maybe he had some wizard blood in him or just was using a device. "Just tell us where our room is!"

He reluctantly pointed to a staircase. "Just go up those stairs and down the hall. It's the last door on the left."
We said our thanks and headed up to our room. "Why did he think that we'd be okay with him unpacking our luggage?" Eddie asked

"That was unsettling," I said as I unlocked our room's door. "Holy Candy Canes, Batman!" I said as I stepped inside.

"Wow!" Eddie was equally impressed. "I didn't realize that a candy cane-themed room was possible."

The bedroom was lined with huge, red, and white vertical striped wallpaper. The king-sized bedspread with little candy canes on a bright green background even had red and white striped pillows. Over the bed hung two crisscrossed giant candy canes which I suspected were leftovers from the tree in the lobby.

I opened the white-painted wardrobe and found the interior painted with more little candy canes on a green background. Someone had even painted a couple of pictures of some candy canes growing out of the snow. Even the brick of the fireplace shared the same color scheme as the rest of the suite.

You'd think that with all the cost poured into this tacky decorating scheme, the hotel would have invested in a matching mini fridge and microwave. But no, the lime green mini-fridge, toaster oven, and microwave all looked like they had a rough time traveling from the 1970s to the present with their huge dents. Even in all its striped glory, the room was freezing cold. I hugged myself as I searched around for a thermostat while Eddie put away my six-pack of fruit dragon blood.

When I finally found it, I had to give them credit. They had cleverly camouflaged the thermostat to match the wallpaper. I did a double-take when I read the temperature. "How is it possible for a room to be colder than outside?"

Eddie looked at the thermostat and then at me. "65 degrees is not that cold, babe."

"Yes, is it," I replied as I turned it up to a toasty 68 degrees. "Remember how cold our room was at the resort where we stayed on our honeymoon?"

"We were staying on a tropical island where it was 75 degrees all year around."

"And yet I was so cold at night, I had to buy a fifty-dollar sweatshirt to keep warm."

"I thought most of the nights were pretty steamy," Eddie mused with a grin.

I playfully slapped his butt. "And how! But I was talking about afterward when the first night got really cold, and I woke up with a headache. Good thing I brought the sweatshirt with us." I knelt and opened our suitcase to retrieve it. "Oh, zamnnit! I left it at home."

"We can ask the front desk to see about turning up the

heat," Eddie said he went into the bathroom to wash up and found even more candy cane-themes in the bathroom. When he came out he was smiling. "Definitely over-the-top on the decor, but the soap smells delicious!"

"Let me guess. Peppermint?"

"Of course!" My wonderful husband knows how much I love scented soaps, especially ones that make you hungry.

"We need to get some at the gift shop for stocking stuffers when I pick up a new sweatshirt!" I paused as a thought popped into my mind. "Eddie, are cervitaurs magical?"

"Not to my knowledge, but he could be. He walked through that wall. Why do you ask?"

"Something was off about him. I just can't put my finger on it."

Eddie shrugged."Then I don't know what to tell you. I just think he was way too enthusiastic about helping us."

I nodded. "There's helpfulness and then there is borderline creepy." I glanced at my phone. "Okay, we're supposed to meet with Ms. Doodleysqueaks in a few minutes at the local pub."

The walk to O'Tannenbaum's was thankfully short in the freezing cold. A little bell rang above us as we entered the pub. "Sit anywhere ya want, and I'll be right with ya," the gruff-looking elf behind the dark cherry counter told us. I was pleasantly surprised with his non-Christmassy outfit which consisted of a simple red and green plaid buttoned-up shirt over a white t-shirt and blue jeans. The shirt was rolled up past the elbows, revealing a dancing snowman tattoo on his left forearm.

As soon as we took off our coats and hats, Eddie and I sat down at one of the forest green pub tables with two dark cherry wooden chairs. "This is nice," I said as I took in the simple, Christmas decor which consisted of a few wreaths with red and green bows mounted here and there on the walls. A tree-shaped jar marked "tips" sat near the cash register.

True to his word, the elf came over to our table. "Welcome to O'Tannenbaum's. Name's Niall," he said pleasantly as he handed us two menus. "Can I start you folks off with something to drink?"

"Yes! Could I get some coffee?" I said.

"Regular peppermint or decaf peppermint?"

"Regular with cream and two sugars, and water as well, please"

Niall turned to Eddie. "You sir?"

"I'll have the same."

He jotted down our drink orders and started to leave the table when I said to him, "Is Ms. Doodleysqueaks here? We're supposed to meet with her."

"No, sorry," he said. "'I don't know who she is."

Eddie and I exchanged perplexed looks. "She's Santa's press secretary," I said.

The elf owner shrugged. "Sorry, ma'am. Never heard of her."

Weird. "Okay, thank you, anyways."

Once he was out of earshot, I said to the vampire. "How could he not know who Santa's press secretary is?"

Eddie shrugged. " He might be new to the town."

"That's a fair point, but it still makes no sense." I looked over the lunch options, and my face brightened when I saw the first one. "Ooh, I'm getting the fish and chips."

"I haven't had fish and chips in decades," my husband said. "But now that I can take Hemoase, I'm going to have some, too." When he was first turned into a vampire, Eddie unfortunately discovered that he is severely allergic to blood because of a rare genetic disorder. If he drinks any blood, he will throw up.

He has been a vegetarian until we met my Minister of Science and Technology, Dr. Charles Wandasen, a paranoid, yet brilliant wizard. Dr. Wandasen took it upon himself to develop a medicine for Eddie to take so he can eat meat again. After many clinical trials with the vampire as a guinea pig, the drug Hemoase was on the market, and now Eddie could eat meat again.

I glanced up from deciding on anything else to see Claude entering the restaurant. The cervitaur waved to us and went behind the counter. Eddie and I looked at each other. "He must work here as well," I said when we both heard muffled shouting from what we assumed was the kitchen.

Then the cervitaur emerged from the counter with a triumphant smile as he swaggered over to our table. "Good news, Your Majesties! I have resolved your problem with Niall charging you for your meals. Everything is on the house!"

I was taken aback. "There's no need for that! We'll gladly pay for our meals."

"Don't bother. I'll be back to escort you to your meeting with Santa."

"No need to, " I said. "We're supposed to meet with Ms. Doodleysqueaks."

Anger flashed across his face, but he quickly pasted a false smile. "Unfortunately, Ms. Doodleysqueaks no longer works for Santa."

"I'm sorry. I wasn't aware of that," I said, trying not to stare at his tongue darting in and out of his mouth. Which should have been normal, except for the fact that the tip was constantly changing from being forked one second and rounded the next. I nudged my husband for him to take a look, but by the time Eddie turned his head, Claude's tongue looked completely normal.

"Not to worry! Rest assured everything is fine once you meet with Santa and his employees. Enjoy your lunch!"

"Thank you," I said, expecting him to leave the pub. Instead, Claude sat down at a table not too far from us, but definitely within earshot, and smiled pleasantly at us. *I don't like him staring at us,* I telepathically told Eddie.

Me neither.

It's like he's spying on us.

But for who?

We stopped our telepathy as soon as Niall arrived with our drinks. The second he saw the cervitaur, his hands began to shake as he tried to keep the drink tray steady. "Have you decided on what you want?" he asked. Both Eddie and I could hear the fear hiding in his pleasant tone. Claude's presence in his establishment was definitely upsetting him.

"Uh, We'll have two orders of fish and chips," I said.

The elf scribbled down our orders and scurried away.

Eddie and I sipped our coffee in awkward silence. My eyes kept drifting over to Claude. The cervitaur's idea of being incognito was looking through two handmade eyeholes of the newspaper he was "reading." I would've laughed at the absurdity, but his mere presence had upset the pub owner.

Not being very subtle, is he? Eddie noted telepathically.

Nope. Something's not right with him. It took years of

practice, but I had finally mastered the art of keeping my face neutral whenever we spoke telepathically with each other.

What do you mean?

I think his tongue was shapeshifting.

Eddie casually glanced over at Claude but saw nothing out of the ordinary. He turned back to me. *His tongue was shapeshifting?*

One second it was rounded, the next it was forked.

Even Eddie couldn't maintain a neutral expression. *Tongues don't shapeshift.*

I shrugged. I'm just telling you what I—. I stopped mid-thought as my attention was suddenly drawn to our empty coffee cups that began to vibrate on the table. "What the frig?" I asked as everything began to shake around us. The shaking lasted only a few moments, and even though I didn't like the guy, I wanted to make sure Claude was alright.

"Are you all right?" I called over to the cervitaur.

He casually lowered the paper he was reading." Why, of course, Your Majesty! Are your drinks not to your liking?"

I was surprised by his answer. "The coffee's great, but I

was concerned about the earthquake."

"What earthquake?"

How could he not feel the tremor? "Uh, the one we just had!"

He gave me a patronizing smile. "I don't know what you're talking about." The unfazed tone in his voice was unsettling. "You must be very exhausted from your trip, Your Majesty."

Eddie was about to get up from his seat to defend me, but I shook my head. I only responded with "okay" as we went back to sipping our coffee.

What the frig was that about? Eddie mentally asked me. I shrugged. *There was an earthquake here a few moments ago, right? I didn't just hallucinate that?*

No hallucinations on your part. There definitely was an earthquake here.

Maybe Ho Hoboken gets so many earthquakes that Claude is used to them.

But his reaction was weird. Seeing Eddie's puzzled reaction, I explained. *If an outsider comments on something that occurs all the time, saying it's weird or something, what would your response be?*

I would most likely explain to them what was going on, Eddie said. His eyes widened as he realized my point. *Because not telling them or flat-out denying it would be crazy.*

I nodded. *Not to mention incredibly irritating to the newcomer.* I casually glanced out the window at the completely ordinary-looking Arctic tern who was sitting in a tree by a snow-covered building across the street. The white bird with the black head began frantically beckoning to me. Not saying another word, I got up from my seat and went outside to investigate.

I had forgotten that I was not in the tropical climate of Peregrin the moment I stepped outside in the frigid air. "Wait!" I called after the bird as it took off into the sky. I saw a tiny rider riding on the back of the bird, but they didn't seem to hear me. "Okay, what was that all about?" I said aloud to the empty street.

Wrapping my arms around myself in a quickly failing attempt to keep warm, I walked to the middle of the street and looked up at O'Tannenbaum's roof and then down at the newly plopped pile of snow. What the frig? How in the world could an earthquake only affect one building and nothing nearby? It didn't make sense.

As I pondered this puzzling predicament, the snow on the roof of the Sugarplum Bakery slid off as the building itself began to shake violently. To my unbelieving eyes, I watched as the rumbling stopped and then moved on to Sargent Peppermint's Mini-Mart next door. Same thing happened. The building shook for a few moments before stopping abruptly. The same bizarre pattern went on for several buildings down the street, before going back the same way. Only one building was affected by each tremor. The extent of my earthquake knowledge was very basic, but even I knew that earthquakes aren't that precise.

"Enjoying our little town, Your Majesty?" asked a skin-crawling voice in my ear.

I spun around to see Claude with his awful-smelling cologne once again invading my personal space. Struggling momentarily for a more diplomatic answer other than "Dude, back it up!" I finally replied with a less-than-perfect answer, "Uh, sure."

Claude inched even closer. "I believe your food is ready,"

he said as he took the crook of my arm.

I tried to conceal my shock, not only at him grabbing me without my permission (Dude, have you no concept of boundaries?) but also at his hand against my skin. The hands were hard, dry, and incredibly scaly. Definitely not what I was expecting at all.

I tried to pull away from him, but he had me in an unexpected vice-like grip. As a vampire, I have the strength of a gorilla or two, but to my horror, I couldn't break free from him. I looked around for Eddie to intervene, but my vampire bodyguard was nowhere in sight. Zamn, I was beginning to wish I hadn't left my sword and shield back in the hotel room. I reluctantly gave in as I had no choice but to allow Claude to force me back inside the restaurant.

I soon realized why Eddie hadn't come outside to help me. I noticed my husband struggling to get up from his seat, but there were no bonds that I could see. One glare at the cervitaur from him told me that something had gone wrong.

Claude yanked out my chair and almost pushed me into it

before shoving me and the chair against the table. Then he took his seat in the same spot as before.

Are you all right? I telepathically asked Eddie.

Don't know.

My eyes widened in surprise. *What do you mean?*

It was weird. The second you left our table--which by the way, what was that all about—I got up, but Claude started to follow you. He put his hand on my shoulder, and I immediately felt compelled to stay where I was. I felt almost glued here.

Same here. I mentally told him about my observation of the weird earthquake and my *uncomfortable* encounter with the cervitaur as we dug into our fish and chips.

That's weird. I can safely say that I've never heard of an earthquake moving in a particular pattern.

And only affecting one small area at a time.

I thought Ho Hoboken would be really fun to visit because of Santa and all, but so far it's been one weird thing after another. To hear that coming from a vampire who has been around for several decades was not at all reassuring. *Come to think of it, most of the really strange things I've ever encountered have always been with you.*

I touched his arm. *And I wouldn't have it any other way.*

We ate in silence. Even though I'm used to telepathic communication, I much prefer talking the old-fashioned way. Unfortunately with Claude hovering over us like a KGB agent, talking aloud about the current situation was not going to happen. I casually glanced at our stalker. *I'm pretty sure he isn't a cervitaur.*

The vampire nodded in agreement. *And before you ask, I don't know who or what Claude really is.*

I smiled. *Look who the mind reader is now.*

Not mind reading, babe, but years of knowing you.

The moment we finished the last tasty morsel, Claude rushed to our table. "All right, Your Majesties, shall we go to the meeting?"

Chapter Three
Jerky Old Saint Nicholas

It was a good ten-minute walk in the bitter cold to the enormous toy factory just on the outskirts of town. There were no fresh sleigh marks in the road, no winged animals of any kind. How did the factory employees commute? I mentioned the absence of transportation to our guide.

"Magic," replied Claude.

"As in teleportation, flying spells?" I asked, hoping for more than just a vague answer than "magic."

"Magic," said the cervitaur again before falling silent.

Wow, he's super helpful, I mentally told Eddie.

He would make a great tour guide. Eddie responded. *Answering questions with such vagueness.*

I was about to make an award-winning comment when we arrived at the football stadium-size toy factory that dwarfed the rest of Ho Hoboken's buildings. I expected to hear your typical hustle and bustle of a global toy-making operation, but even with my vampire hearing, it was awfully quiet.

Toxic, plastic-infused smoke should have been billowing out of the inactive eight red and white smokestacks on top of the silver and gold building. The large sign for the Toy Factory was covered in a thin layer of ice and had not been turned on in quite some time. Snow had piled up in the front of the public entrance doors.

Claude forcefully guided us to the back of the building. This excursion took an additional fifteen minutes of walking falling multiple times on the snow-covered ice. Once the cervitaur opened the steel door for us, I hobbled inside and brushed the snow off of my pants. I shuddered from the cold. Someone had forgotten to pay their heating bill. How could a building be colder than the outside?

A disappointed look appeared on my husband's face as we looked around the vast, silent factory floor. Giantatic robotic arms hung in mid-movement over ten large, long conveyor belts that were either empty or had a few toys scattered here and there. Claude definitely didn't know how to read a room as he mistook Eddie's shock for awe. "The toy designs are inputed into one of the Stocking Stuffers and out comes a toy!" He pointed to a huge red machine at the front of a conveyor belt.

"What happened there?" Eddie asked, pointing to a huge, gaping hole in the machine's side that clearly wasn't part of the design. Someone's idea of fixing it involved covering it halfway up with poinsettia-themed wrapping paper and tape and slapping a big red bow in the middle.

The cervitaur looked directly at the machine. "Whatever are you talking about?"

My husband walked over to inspect the Stocking Stuffer. "It looks like your machine is damaged. I'm a pretty good mechanic, and I could repair it for you guys."

Claude raced over to stand in front of the hole. "The machine is fine. There is nothing wrong with it."

Eddie shook his head. "Look, it's no issue. I'll be happy to help you guys out."

The cervitaur stood his ground as he gave a fake laugh. "I don't know what you're talking about, your Majesty. This oddity didn't faze the cervitaur as he continued with the impromptu tour. "Elves monitor the toy from the machine down the end of the conveyor belt where our present wrapping experts are hard at work." He waved to nonexistent people at a table cluttered with wrapping paper, ribbons, bows, tape dispensers, and scissors.

There is no one at that table, right? I mentally asked Eddie.

Not a single person. I can't decide what makes me more disappointed. Santa's workshop looks like an abandoned factory you'd see on a reality TV show or our tour guide thinks this place is up and running.

"How do the designs get made, you ask? That job belongs to our toy artists." He pointed to a room with sheetrock walls and plexiglass windows directly across from the defunct Stocking Stuffer. "After we receive a prechixild's- I mean, child's-letter to Santa describing their toy, our toy artists draw an image of the toy in what we call the 'Imaginavision Room.' As you can see, the elves are painstakingly, hard at work in this soundproof room."

There were three very incorrect things Claude said. One, the room held only overturned easels and drawing utensils scattered across the floor, but no people. Two, the hubcap-sized gear embedded in the back wall of the room indicated the room was no longer soundproof as did the matching hole in the plexiglass window. The third thing was the strange word he said. I had never heard before, "prechixild." The cervitaur had corrected himself so quickly that I almost missed it. Attributing it to the man's nervousness, I shrugged it off as we ascended some metal stairs overlooking the factory floor.

"The meeting will be in the conference room," Claude told us as he pointed to an ajar door just to the left of the staircase. He guided us inside and then left with the door firmly closed behind him.

The blandness of the conference room compared to the rest of Ho Hoboken surprised both Eddie and myself. Beige walls surrounded an equally beige table and eight chairs. I chose a seat closest to the back of the room. "Is it me or is this place getting weirder by the minute?" I asked.

Eddie sat next to me. "Unless the elves are invisible, no one has been working in this factory for a while." He let out a disappointed sigh. "I really wanted to see how Santa's operation worked."

"If we save Christmas, you might get your chance."

A lanky blond elf in a red jumpsuit entered the room and sat down at the opposite end of the table. He gave us a curt nod as he crossed his arms over his chest. His steel-toed boots thudded on the table as he put up his feet.

"I'm Queen Shelly Van Helsing, and this is King Eddie Van Helsing."

The elf nodded but decided not to share his name with us. He retrieved his phone from his pocket and focused all his attention on it. Great! What a super warm reception!

The door opened and an eight-foot-tall yeti ducked through the doorway. I had only seen a sasquatch once in my life, but that was only a shape-shifting genie. This one was the real thing. The green short-sleeved shirt showed off the bugling muscles of his white furry arms. Under the golden Ho Hoboken Security badge was a nameplate that read "Bartholomew." His huge, ape-like feet stuck out from the ends of his neatly pressed black pants. The white fur around his head was slicked from his Neanderthal-like face. "Guy," he said to the elf with a snarl as he sandwiched himself into a chair.

"Bartholomew," Guy replied icily.

Eddie and I glanced at each other but said nothing to break the tension in the room. After about three more minutes of awkward silence that I had to break, I introduced Eddie and myself to Bartholomew. I was met with more silence. This was going great.

Thankfully, the door opened, and in walked Claude and the man with all the toys himself. Santa looked exactly as I'd pictured him. A bald, portly man with a big white beard and rosy cheeks. Gold-framed spectacles sat perched on the edge of his very red nose. He wasn't wearing the classic suit, though. Instead, he wore bright green sweatpants, sneakers, and to top it all, a Christmas sweater that read, "Mrs. Claus puts the 'ho' in 'ho, ho, ho.'"

Now, I understand people grieve in different ways, but for someone whose loved one is missing, the sweater was very distasteful. I hid my surprise as Claude introduced everyone in the room. The elf, Guy Elfstrong, was the head toymaker, and the yeti, Bartholemew, was the head of security. "I'm sorry to hear about Mrs. Claus," I said to Santa.

"It is what it is," Santa said with a shrug. "I don't need that old hag."

Yeah, Mrs. Claus just didn't just disappear. He totally killed her. Santa sat down beside us, and the smell of alcohol and the same terrible cologne nearly overwhelmed me. That's why the nose was red. I put aside my surprise and addressed everyone. "I was asked to help mediate a disagreement here in Ho Hoboken. I want to hear all sides before--."

"I can tell you exactly what happened," Guy interrupted me as he jabbed a finger at Bartholemew. "This incompetent cryptid and his so-called security team weren't doing their jobs when Mrs. Claus disappeared."

"I wasn't the one who was in charge when the explosion happened!" shouted Bartholemew.

"He's right, you know," Santa said to me casually.

"What?" I asked as I quickly turned to him. A huge grin

flashed across Santa's face. Was he enjoying this fighting or just really drunk? Then he blinked his eyes which horrified me as some kind of clear membrane ran across each eyeball.

What the frig? Eddie telepathically asked me. Good, he had seen it, too. I wasn't hallucinating.

"You know Guy hates sasquatches. He thinks that only elves should be allowed in the toy factory." The subtle, disembodied voice whispered in Bartholemew's ear, but my vampiric hearing picked it up. I glanced around for the source but found nothing.

"My team and I put our lives on the line for your ungrateful hides every day! That's why my brother's missing."

I heard the same disembodied voice this time whispering in Guy's ear. "You don't need any sasquatch help. All they do is stand around and look tough."

"I don't even know why Santa hired you sasquatches," Guy yelled at Bartholomew. "You don't do a zamn thing!"

It was at this point both the elf and the yeti started arguing with each other as both Eddie and I tried to regain control of the situation. We gave up thirty minutes into the fight. The most irritating thing was Santa. He just sat back with a maniacal grin and just watched the whole thing evolve into a dumpster fire.

Santa decided to take action an hour later. "Alright! This is progress," he said happily. "We should prerixecixonvixonixe--I mean, reconvene, tomorrow morning at nine." He got up and quickly left the room with his lackey, Claude, behind him.

The rest of us awkwardly followed them and stopped short at the railing. "Get back to work, you lazy clods!" Santa yelled down at the nonexistent workers. He looked at me. "Do you ever have these kinds of problems with employees?" he asked me with all seriousness.

I shook my head. "Can't say I have." Because I don't yell at empty workstations. One look at Guy and Bartholomew told me that even though something was very wrong, they sure weren't going to interfere with the craziness.

Instead, we all followed Santa out of the factory and went our separate ways. Except for Claude. He insisted on guiding us back to the Holly Jolly Inn. At first, I thought he was going to attempt to pry information out of us, but I was wrong.

"Isn't Santa the most wonderful person ever?" he gushed.

Not exactly what I was thinking. Fortunately, my years as a former library assistant listening to crazy people came to my rescue. "Uh-huh," I replied.

"Rather convincing, don't you think?" the cervitaur asked.

Eddie immediately suspected something was not right. My husband stopped in his tracks. "Say what?" he asked as he narrowed his eyes on Claude.

Panic spread across his face as the cervitaur obviously said something he shouldn't have. "I-I--must go!" He quickly ran off in the opposite direction.

"What was that all about?" I asked.

"I have no idea, but there's a lot of bizarre things going on around here."

We started hurrying back to the hotel as white specks started to fall from the twilight sky. A small rustle of leaves caught my attention, and I whipped my head around to locate the sound. We were the only ones on the empty street.

"Everything okay, babe?" Eddie asked.

I frowned as I looked around. "I thought I heard something behind us."

My husband took a look around. "I don't see anyone. Do you think someone is following us?"

"Not sure," I replied. I blew out a sigh as I started walking again. Maybe the freezing temperatures were causing me to have auditory hallucinations. "Have you noticed how quiet the town is?"

"You'd think Ho Hoboken would be bustling a few days before Christmas."

"Instead, it feels like a ghost town." No children played in the streets. Curtains were drawn and lights were off in every house. There were no stirring creatures as far as Eddie and I could see.

When we arrived at our room, I spotted something attached to the door's bottom. It was a small sticky note with the word help written on it. I picked it up and turned it over looking for a signature, but the back was blank.

"What's that?" Eddie asked as he unlocked the door.

"Don't know. All it says is help."

"I wondered who wrote it?"

"With all the strangeness in this place, it could be from anyone."

The smell of fresh flowers filled the room the moment we walked in. Two bouquets of assorted wildflowers sat on the large TV stand. "Beautiful flowers, Eddie. You really know how to make a woman feel special." I said.

My husband smiled. "I wish I could take the credit, but I didn't do this."

The enthusiasm deflated from me like a balloon. I let out a sigh as I took the small envelope from the small pick sticking out from one of the vases. "Maybe I've got a secret admirer." I started to read the note as a grimace appeared on my face. "What's up with people always trying to bribe me? Do I have a bribable face or something?"

"Rachel was probably easily bribed, and people must think you are too," Eddie surmised.

"I wish people would stop comparing me to my sister." My younger sister, Rachel, and I might be twins, but aside from being queens, we are nothing alike. She tried to kill me multiple times. One of those times she actually did and turned me into a vampire. She also was a tyrannical queen who ruled with an iron fist. The citizens of Peregrin were probably going to feel the effects of her rule for years to come. "I'm nothing like her, and I never will be."

Eddie put his arms around me. "You're a great queen, Shell, who cares about her citizens." He kissed the top of my head. This is one of the many reasons why I love him. "What does the note say?" Eddie asked.

" 'The elves are in the wrong.' I suspect the other note says something similar about the sasquatches."

Eddie nodded as he got the other note. "Yep." I shook my head in anger as I wondered how many times Rachel had accepted bribes. Probably every time. "I'm going down to the lobby to send these guys a message that I will make my own, friging decision without the use of pathetic bribery."

My husband could tell I was about to go ballistic and decided to be the voice of reason. "Or we could just go back to the pub for supper and tell them in the morning," he suggested.

I gave in with a sigh as my stomach growled. Food did sound like a good idea. "Fine."

As Eddie locked our room door, we saw a little elfin girl chasing a pink-and-green catnip dragon down the hall. "Pinkerton, get back here!" The giggling girl called after the bounding cat-dragon chased the red dot coming from the laser in her hand.

The pet spread its pink butterfly wings and launched itself at my chest. Having dealt with Alonzo playing parkour on me and Eddie, I quickly caught Pinkerton and held the little dragon in my arms. "Hi, there!"

"Thanks, lady," the little girl said as she ran up to us. "Pinkerton likes to catch the red dot."

"Our catnip dragon loves to play that game too," I said as I passed Pinkerton back to her

The girl's purple eyes grew wide with excitement. "You have a catnip dragon, too? What's her name? Did you bring her with you?"

"His name is Alonzo, and unfortunately, no. He had to stay at home."

"Oh, I could never leave Pinkerton. My mommy got her for

me when she was still in her egg." She hugged the wiggly dragon. "She's my second bestest friend in the whole world. Bluebell is my bestest friend in the whole wide world."

"I bet they are," I said.

"But Mommy says Pinkerton can't run up and down the halls because it'll make the guests upset."

She was the owner's daughter. "It could, but we won't tell your mom," Eddie said with a smile. "I'm Eddie and this is Shelly. What's your name?"

"Florence, and I'm seven and three-quarters," she said. Pinkerton began to playfully swat at one of her brown pigtails, and she set the catnip dragon down on the floor. A troubled look appeared on Florence's face. "Are you here to help Santa?" It was an odd question coming from such a young kid. I didn't want to say either way, but I was curious. "Does Santa need help?"

She nodded. "He doesn't give me candy anymore and talks in a funny voice."

"A funny voice?"

She nodded. "Santa used to give all the kids candy, but

since Mrs. Claus went away, he just yells at the kids. One time, I was playing with Pinkerton near Santa's office, and he and Mr. Claude were talking to someone with funny voices."

"You mean you didn't understand what they were saying?"

Florence fervently nodded her head. "Yes, ma'am, but Santa and Mr. Claude were really mean to me. They called me a bad word for hearing them."

Eddie looked at me, and without reading his mind, I knew exactly what he was thinking. Santa and Claude were definitely speaking in a different language. It made sense as we were talking about the man who delivers toys to kids around the world, but why were they trying to hide it? Santa calling a kid a dirty word? That didn't sound like the Santa I knew about growing up. Something smelled in Ho Hoboken, and it wasn't gingerbread.

Chapter Four:
Someone's Halls Got Decked

After saying goodbye to Florence, Eddie and I walked to O'Tannenbaum's in the cold. "The nightlife here isn't stimulating at all," I remarked as I noticed how empty the streets were.

"Maybe everyone's at the pub," Eddie suggested.

"Something about this town is off."

Eddie nodded. "I would say the townspeople are worried about the tremors, and that Santa's going postal on them."

It seemed to me Ho Hoboken was once a happy place but since Mrs. Claus went missing, all that had obviously changed. Everyone Eddie and I had spoken with was on edge. Ho

Hoboken reminded me of when I took over as queen of Peregrin.

I temporarily pushed Ho Hobeken's troubles to the back of my mind when we felt the earth shake under us. The sudden tremor was so violent that we lost our footing and fell back into a nearby snowbank. "You all--" My concerned question was cut off as we saw an object that looked like a body shoot up in the air followed by flying dirt and land under one of the many lighted evergreens lining the street. "Holy crap! What the frig was that?"

Eddie scrambled to his feet first and then helped me to mine. He looked at me with a knowing smile. "Don't know, but I take it you want to investigate?"

"Of course!" I said as I hurried over.

My assumption was right. I stared down at the shriveled-up body before us. The poor soul looked like it had been mummified, and that wasn't even the most disturbing thing about it. Whatever happened to this person had completely turned them, including their clothes, into a drab brown color.

A gasp came from Eddie "Holy crap! It's the owner of the pub!" he said.

"How can you tell?"

The vampire squatted down in the snow. "I recognized the tattoo." He pointed to a barely visible dancing snowman on the body's forearm.

I squatted down to get a closer look, and the hem of my coat sleeve brushed against the body. A loud hissing noise erupted from the dead man's mouth. "What the frig!" I swore as I recoiled back in surprise.

"What did you do?" Eddie asked as we both watched in shock as the corpse imploded on itself like a deflating balloon.

I held my hands up. "Nothing!"

"Move!" my husband ordered. He pulled me away from the expected flying of organs and bodily fluids. But the only thing that came out was a foul-smelling cloud of dust.

We looked at each other and then down at the body which was now as flat as a dried pancake. "Uh, shouldn't there be blood and gore?" I asked.

Eddie nodded. "Usually."

Because I had no clue who or what could have literally flattened a person I racked my brain for any information about what could have done this. I looked to my husband for answers. I didn't even need to read his mind to know that he knew as much as I did just by the confused look on his face. "Okay, next question," I said hesitantly. "Where did the body come from?" I asked.

"Maybe from there?" Eddie suggested as he pointed to an object further up the street.

I followed him over. "Well, that's new," I said as Eddie and I peered down the dark gaping hole in the ground. Which was a terrible mistake as a foul smell hit our noses so hard it made both our eyes water. "Oh, god! It smells like rotten meat down there" I said, trying not to gag. I took several steps back.

My husband covered his nose with his hand as he joined me. "Yeah, and a lot of it."

"How the frig is that possible in this freezing cold weather?"

"No idea."

Loud clicks echoed up from somewhere deep inside the hole. I had heard strange noises before, but this one gave me the chills that had nothing to do with the winter weather. Normally, I would want to investigate, but my gut was screaming no. "I would say let's see what's down there, but since our weapons are back in our room, let's not risk our lives needlessly."

"Only risk them with our weapons?"

"You know me well." I glanced at the pub ahead of us. "I'm not hungry, but we should let people know about poor Niall here."

Eddie nodded in agreement. "Yeah, seeing a flattened body void of all of its internal organs has made me lose my appetite, too."

O'Tannenbaum's was just as empty as it was at lunchtime. The only people in the pub were Claude and Santa, hunched over a small booth in the back with a blob of green goo sitting in the middle of the table. Serious health code violation right there!

Now, let me preface by saying, that I don't eavesdrop, but I can hear the slightest whisper because of my vampiric hearing. The strange thing was I couldn't even understand what they were saying as they kept looking over at me and Eddie.

"Prehixavixe preyixoixu prefixoixund prethixem preyixet?" Santa asked Claude.

"Prenixo, precixolixonixel," replied the cervitaur. "Prei prehixavixe prelixoixokixed preevixerywhixerixe prefixor prethixem."

"Prewixe preonly prehixavixe prethrixeixe premixorixe predixays prebixefixorixe Ziggurart prearrixivixes. If prehixe prefiixnds preoixut--"

The blob began to shake and move slowly as a disembodied voice joined their conversation. "Prewhixat preis preyixoixur prerixepixort, Damien?"

"Prewixe prehixavixe prenixot prelixocixatixed prethixe pretrixaiixtixors, pregixenixerixal," Santa replied, visibly nervous.

"Predixid Prei prenixot premixakixe premy preordixers preclixeixar, Damien," the disembodied voice boomed. "Preor prearixe preyixoixu prejixust prea prebixuffixoixon?"

Both Santa and Claude clamored out of their seats and began bowing to the moving blob. "Prelixeixasixe, prehixavixe premixercy preon preus, Pregixenixerixal Ziggurat!" The cervitaur's voice had changed from confident to terrified.

"Pregixenixerixal, preit preixis prenixot preixas preixeixasy preixas preyixoixu prethixiink," Santa said. "Prethixerixe prehixavixe prebixeixen precixomplixicixatixixions."

Do you know what they are saying? I telepathically asked
Eddie.

My husband stared at me in shock as he looked up from
his phone. *I can't believe you're eavesdropping!*

*It's not eavesdropping if you don't know what the other
people are saying.*

He blew out a sigh, knowing that once again I was right.
No, I don't speak any other languages.

I raised my eyebrows in pretend shock. *I thought every
tough spy was a multilinguist. I'm shocked!*

Sorry to disappoint you.

I grinned at him. *Well, you're still my favorite tough guy.
While you were staring at them-you've got to work on being
subtle, babe-I've been recording their conversation.* Eddie
casually showed me the voice memo he had been so subtly
recording.

Good thinking, hon. That's why I keep you around.

The disembodied voice thundered. "Prethixen pretixakixe
precixarixe preof prethixosixe precixomplixicixatiiuxixons!

Predixo prenixot precixontixact premixe preagixaixin preunixtil preyixoixu prehixavixe preapprixehixendixed prethixe prertrixaiixtixors!"

"Preyixes, presiixr!" Santa said he sloppily saluted the moving blob which responded with a loud splat back on the table.

I waited with bated breath to see if the blob would move again. Crazy, I know, but I was fully invested. The blob remained still, and my mind flooded with multiple questions. What exactly was the blob? Was it a person, animal, or mineral? Why did Santa salute it? Why did it scare both of them? What were they saying to it?

"Shelly!" Eddie's elbow nudged me in the side bringing me back to reality.

"I'm sorry. You were saying Santa?"

The jerky old man had gotten up from his seat and rushed over to us. "Your Majesties, it's so great to see you again! I trust your stay has been merry?" He gave an obvious fake ho-ho.

I love dad jokes, and I can make puns with the best of them. But Santa's ever-changing disposition was incredibly disconcerting. His moods changed at the same if not faster, rate than a set of color-changing twinkle lights set to music. "Santa, we have something important to tell you," I said.

"Have you been a naughty girl?" he said with a wink. Oh, for frig's sake! I resisted the strong temptation to give myself a facepalm. "Santa, something killed the pub's owner!" I said. A huge grin spread across the old man's face. "Why, whatever are you talking about?"

As soon as I explained to him what Eddie and I found, he burst out laughing for a good minute. Not the reaction we were expecting. "I didn't realize the queen liked to pull pranks. You must be a prehixoixot at parties."

In what world do people pull pranks about someone's death? Maybe Old Saint Nick was the type of person who needed to see it to believe it. "Mr. Claus, I think you really needed to see this!" I insisted.

"Of course, your Majesty," Santa said with a laugh. "Niall!" he yelled towards the kitchen.

I looked at Eddie incredulously. *Um, did I just say we found the pub owner's body?* I asked him telepathically.

The vampire nodded. *But he wasn't paying attention.*

A short, chubby elf wearing the same outfit Niall had been wearing earlier emerged from the kitchen. He even had the same tattoo, even though it had been hastily drawn on with a permanent marker. "Yes, Santa," he said quickly as he snapped to attention.

"The queen and king think you're dead. Do you want to see your dead body?"

Niall Two quickly shook his head as he put on a plastered smile. "I'm Niall the owner, and I am definitely not dead." He hesitated for only a moment, but after one look at Santa, he quickly added with a nervous chuckle. "I would love to see my dead body."

What the frig was wrong with Santa? I certainly didn't remember the man with the sack being a sadist in folklore. The horrified look on Eddie's face told me that neither did he. I did my best to de-escalate the uncomfortable situation. "Niall doesn't have to come. He has a lot of customers' orders to fulfill."

"Nonsense, it'll be fun!" Santa insisted.

Fun for whom? Other than sadistic jagweeds like

yourself? I thought. Eddie and I reluctantly led the group to where the flattened body lay undisturbed in the snow. The moment Niall Two saw it, he turned and retched on the ground. Claude did the same exact thing, but it was Santa's reaction that took me by surprise.

"Your Majesty, I must confess," Santa said in between huge, full-on belly laughs. "You really had me going there for a moment!"

"What do you mean?" I asked.

He pointed a shaking finger at the body. "I don't see a body, just a snowbank. Isn't that right, Niall?"

The elf had stopped vomiting and slowly nodded his head. "There is no body here, Santa, sir," he said weakly.

Claude pulled himself together and looked at Eddie and me. A stern look appeared in his watery eyes. "How dare you tell lies to Santa! There is no body here! You're on the naughty list!"

Santa put a hand on the cervitaur's shoulder. "Now, Claude, I'm sure the queen and king meant no harm. They're just pulling our prelixegs--I mean, legs."

"Okay," I said, not quite sure what was going on with

these three residents of Ho Hoboken. "The king and I saw it fly up out of that hole over there!"

"What hole?" Santa asked.

"The giant hole that smells like rotten meat over there, "Eddie said as he pointed toward it.

.   "I don't see any holes except for the ones on your faces." Claude laughed as Niall Two smiled nervously.

"There is no body and no hole near us, Santa, sir." the elf said robotically.

Santa chuckled at the vampire. "When you guys pull a prank, you sure are dedicated to it."

I let out an aggravated sigh of defeat. "Never mind. Just forget about it!" I walked back to the pub with everyone trailing behind me.

Back inside, Eddie and I sat down at the same table we were at for lunch. Niall Two hurried over to us and asked us for our orders without even giving us a menu to look at. I quickly thought of a way to help the flustered man as I recalled the soup and salad selections from earlier. "I'll have your curried vegetable chickpea soup with a side of chicken Caesar salad with a sweet tea, please," I said.

Niall Two just stared off into space without writing anything down, creating an uncomfortable moment between us. Finally, he snapped out of it, and fumbled around his pockets until he found a tiny stub of a chewed-on pencil.."I'm sorry. I don't seem to have any paper."

Eddie came to his rescue. He pulled out his wallet. "Here, you can use the back of this," my husband said as he handed the elf an old, crumpled-up receipt."

"Thank you so much," Niall Two said. "I'm not used to working here," he said in a voice, barely above a whisper. The stench of vomit lingered on his breath. He hunched over the table paper with the pencil hovering over the paper.

The elf had completely forgotten my order. I didn't blame him, especially with his visceral reaction to the flattened body. I repeated my order for him and waited patiently as he scribbled it down on the paper. Once he was done with this long process, he asked Eddie for his order.

"I'll have the same thing as my wife," my husband said. Having worked at my dad's restaurant, the vampire knew all about waiting tables and was sympathetic to Niall Two's distress. He wanted to make it as easy as possible for the elf. We both watched as the elf mouthed a word of thanks before scurrying off to the kitchen.

I leaned over to the table and said in a voice only Eddie could hear, "Wow! This is definitely not what I expected Ho Hoboken to be like at all!"

"What? A crazy Santa, flattened bodies, and unexplained earthquakes never graced your Christmas folklore?"

"Shockingly, no. Then again, never in my wildest dreams would I have thought to be turned into a vampire, much less married to one." I placed my hand over his and stroked his cool skin. Unlike Santa here, if Eddie or I ever went missing, we would scour the earth nonstop until the other one was found, and god, help the people responsible!

Our romantic moment was ruined by the front door being slammed shut. We looked out the window in time to see Niall Two running across the street to Sargent Peppermint's Mini-Mart. A few minutes later, he sprinted back to the pub holding a plastic bag.

My phone buzzed in my purse. Once I fished it out, I read the text message from Gunther who was taking care of our catnip dragon with Dusty.

Gunther: Sorry to bother you, Your Majesty. I have a question about the nutritional yeast in Alonzo's bag. What's it for?

Me: You put it on his dry food. He loves it!

Gunther: Okay. How is your trip?

Me: Weird.

Gunther: That wasn't the word I was expecting to hear.

Me: Eddie and I will Facetime you guys later with more information. When's a good time?

Gunther: Tonight around 6:30?

Me: Works for us. How's Alonzo?

Gunther: Good. He was very happy to see us with his food.

"Who are you texting?" Eddie asked me.

I looked up from my phone. "Gunther. He wanted to know what the nutritional yeast was for."

"I must admit even I was skeptical when you started putting it on his food."

I shrugged. "I read about it somewhere when we first got Alonzo." My phone buzzed again. This time the text was from Dusty. It was a picture of the catnip dragon rubbing up against the satyr's legs with the caption: Look who won over Gunther! I let out a laugh as I showed Eddie.

"And Gunther said he wasn't a fan of catnip dragons," Eddie laughed. "I see a catnip dragon or two in their future."

I nodded. Between the couple, Dusty was the one who enthusiastically offered to pet-sit Alonzo while we were away. He had been strongly suggesting to his boyfriend about them getting at least two, "so they can be friends" as Dusty put it. Alonzo, on the other hand, prefers to be the only catnip dragon in our house. "It was only a matter of time."

Niall Two came hurrying out of the kitchen to our table. Our drinks sloshed around in their glasses and the soup splashed out of the bowl as he attempted to set the tray on our table. It was a terrible attempt as my soup bowl tipped over and lukewarm soup spilled on my shirt.

Instantly, Santa and Claude surrounded him. They glared at him with emotionless faces. "Niall, what have you done?" Santa asked him in a tone that betrayed his concern.

Niall Two looked at Santa and me with a horrified expression. He grabbed a napkin from the napkin dispenser. "I'm so so so sorry! Please have mercy!" It wasn't clear if he was talking to me and Eddie or Santa and Claude.

I held up a hand to prevent him from cleaning up the soup from my clothes. "No worries. It was just an accident," I assured Niall Two as I began to wipe off the soup with my napkin.

"Are you sure?" Santa asked. He looked over at my husband. "What are your thoughts on Niall's grave mistake, sire?"

"It's just soup," Eddie said, glancing at me with an incredulous look in his eyes. *You'd think this guy just tried to kill you or something with the way they're carrying on,* he telepathically told me

I know, right? Could you text Gunther that audio file to see

if he can translate it for us?

Sure. The vampire took out his phone and discreetly sent our private secretary the audio file with the message: Shelly and I need some help with this. He looked out the window, and his eyes widened in surprise. "What the frig is that?"

For a moment, I thought he was trying to distract Santa and Claude away from our table but quickly realized that was not the case as Niall Two let out a shriek and ran away to the kitchen like a frightened toddler. I turned around in my chair just in time to see something long and thin disappear behind the roofs of the building across the street. With the several spikes protruding from its head, it looked a lot like the creature I had seen in my dream. I shuddered as a chill went up my spine. That thing, whatever it was, was dangerous.

Apparently, Santa and Claude weren't on the same wavelengths as me. Both the looks on the old man and the weasel-thing's face were ones of irritation, not fear. Without any explanation, they ran out the door, leaving Eddie and I by ourselves in what was becoming a perpetual state of confusion.

"What's wrong, babe?" Eddie asked me the moment he

saw my face.

"That thing! I saw it in my dream last night!"

Eddie nodded grimly. "Frig," he said quietly. "And no, I've never seen anything like that in my life."

"Double frig!" I said. We sat in silence, contemplating our next move. Despite everything, my stomach told me it was time to eat. I looked at my bowl and was very surprised to discover it was pureed. Eddie has made amazing curried vegetable chickpea soup before, and it never looks like this. I tentatively took a sip of it and frowned. "I'm pretty sure this is canned soup."

Eddie took a spoonful of his. "And I recognize the taste. It's the Soup Company's Veggie Curry!"

I grimaced as I knew exactly what he was talking about. When we were first dating, I made soup for dinner one night. Because my cooking skills were about the same level as a two-year-old, I had just reheated two cans of this exact soup. Whoever made this soup must have never heard of the words "spices." It was the blandest thing I've tasted. I've gotten a little better with my culinary skills over the years, and fortunately, I married a fantastic cook.

I ate some more of the bland soup, hoping some magical seasoning had appeared in the past few seconds. Still bland. I pushed the soup aside and started on the salad which definitely tasted like your run-of-the-mill prepackaged grocery store salad, but was pretty good. I suspected that our tea was also picked up from the nearby store. I glanced at the kitchen door, but there was still no sign of Niall Two. "Should we check on him?" I asked Eddie.

My husband looked up from dumping a copious amount of salt onto his soup. "Who?"

"Niall Two."

Is that what you're calling him?" Eddie said as he finally set the salt shaker down. He stirred the soup and took a sip. "Blech! How can something be so bland that salt doesn't affect it?"

"Until we find out his actual name, then yes." I pointed at his salad with my fork. "The salad is pretty good for a general store. Poor Niall Two. Imagine being thrown into an uncertain position like this."

Eddie nodded as he abandoned the soup to start on his

salad. "Judging by his reaction outside, he must have been pretty close with Niall One. He also knows exactly what happened to him."

I got up from my chair. "I'm going to the kitchen to check in on Niall Two and get some answers. You want to come?"

"Sure." We both walked towards the kitchen door. Eddie slowly pushed it open in case something bad was on the other side. We found Niall Two breathing raggedly as he leaned on one of the counters.

"Frig! Frig!" He repeated over and over again.

"Is everything all right?" I asked.

The elf looked up at us, his eyes brimming with tears. "Please forgive me, Your Majesties."

"For what?" I asked.

"For this," he answered as he vaguely gestured around the kitchen. "Niall is-I mean, was-the cook in the family. I'm just the bookkeeper." When Eddie and I didn't correct him, he knew the gig was up. "My name's not Niall," he finally admitted. "It's Chester. Niall was my brother."

"We had a feeling that you weren't named Niall," I said.

"You know what really happened to him, don't you."

"The sworm got him," Chester whispered.

"What's that?" Eddie asked.

"I don't know. It showed up here right after the UFO landed behind the sleigh storage shed."

I raised a skeptical eyebrow. "Did you just say a UFO landed here?"

Chester nodded vigorously. "Yes, it happened right before Mrs. Claus vanished and Claude showed up."

Oh, this trip was getting better and better. I've lived in this magical realm for almost nine years, and I was pretty sure that aliens from another planet don't exist. I didn't say anything to upset the elf.

"I know it sounds crazy, but Santa and Claude summoned the sworm with a jingle bell before feeding Niall to it. They did it to Denise Doodleysqueaks, and they'll do it again."

"Wow!" I said, shocked at what I was hearing. Santa had crossed the line from a jerk to a murdering psychopath. "Is there anything we can do?"

"Leave Ho Hoboken and never look back!"

Okay, that kind of warning was usually reserved for Old Man Harbinger of Doom horror movie cliche. Just like the unwitting town newcomers, my husband and I didn't listen to him. "No," I said, "We're here to help!"

The kitchen swung open and in walked Santa and Claude. A look of paranoia appeared on Santa's face the moment he saw Chester talking to us. "Niall, were the king and queen not pleased with your meal?"

The elf tried to speak, but fear held his tongue. I could hear his heart beating rapidly as he gripped the counter for support. His purple eyes looked at me for help.

"Actually, we were just complimenting Niall on the excellent food he made for us," I immediately interjected.

Eddie nodded. "His curry vegetable chickpea soup was the best I've ever tasted." It was not true, but my husband would rather tell a lie to save Chester's life.

"I'm sure." The tone in Santa's voice made me rethink my words. Did my facial expressions betray me and doom Chester? "I need to have a private word with Niall here. Claude, escort the king and queen back to their table."

We didn't have a choice as the cervitaur used the same force spell on us. Once he placed a hand on each one of Eddie's and my shoulders, he literally shoved us through the kitchen doors and back to our seats. "Don't move or else!" He threatened us before returning to the kitchen.

We struggled against our invisible bonds, but whatever magic Claude had used had been metaphorically glued to our seats. I tried to wiggle out of my seat for a few seconds but realized my terrible mistake as the chair tipped backward. I landed on the floor with a loud thud. "Ow!"

Eddie peered around the edge of the table. "You okay?"

"Aside from a possible concussion, I'm fine." I rocked myself back and forth in a failed attempt to upright myself. I stopped when I heard my husband snickering.

"You look like a helpless beetle on its back," he said as evenly as he could muster.

"Hilarious. Now, have you figured out a way to break this binding spell?"

"I'm trying." The former wizard reached deep into the recesses of his mind for a way to free us. A confused look spread over his face which is never a good sign. "I can't. We're not dealing with magic here."

I looked over at him in shock. "It's not? What are you talking about?"

"Whenever people use magic, I can sense it."

My husband could spot magic being used at any time, but I couldn't, even after becoming a vampire. I wondered if it was because of his ancestry. Eddie was born a Welkie, a race of long-living human-like people who can perform magical spells. They are known as wizards and enchantresses, but those who use dark magic call themselves sorcerers and witches. When Eddie was turned into a vampire, he retained some of his Welkie magic. I ignored my throbbing headache for a chance to learn more. I could already feel myself healing. "Kind of like some kind of spidey sense?"

"Something like that. With whatever this is, I can't sense anything at all."

Our conversation was cut short by a loud scuffle behind the closed kitchen door. There was a muffled scream which was followed by a door slamming shut. Another tremor rumbled through the pub which didn't help my head at all.

Whatever was sealing us to our chairs had vanished, and I scrambled to my feet and touched the back of my head. Ooh, that hurt! Good thing my speedy healing abilities were already kicking in, but I was definitely going to down an entire bottle of fruit dragon blood back at the hotel.

My husband was already at the kitchen door and tried to open it. "Frig! It's locked!" he said. He backed up and was about to kick it open when I stopped him.

"Uh, Eddie, just turn into mist and go under the door. No need to be destructive."

"Good idea," he said. The vampire changed into a green mist and darted under the door. Seconds later, he opened it and let me inside the kitchen.

"Wow!" I said, taking in the mess before us. We stepped over scattered kitchen utensils and broken plates and dishes as we made our way to the employee emergency exit. Fortunately for us, it wasn't locked. I opened it to see a set of five-clawed weasel tracks and boot tracks flanking drag marks in the snow.

Frig! Santa and Claude must have overpowered Chester

and were dragging him off to who knows where. "Come on!" I said to Eddie.

"Aren't you the least bit concerned that we don't have our weapons with us?" the vampire asked.

I grinned. "Nah! We've got your magic and my ability to turn into a black panther. We're good!"

"Okay!" Eddie replied, not entirely convinced. He has been with me long enough to know that once I set my mind to something, there's no stopping me for a while.

We followed the trail for about a hundred feet when I noticed that the tracks were changing shape. Not from the lightly falling snow, but both sets of tracks went from boot and cloven hoofprints to two sets of strange-looking prints. Whatever had made these tracks had five long toes on each foot and left a long thin trail that dragged in the snow.

I crouched down for a closer look when I felt someone watching us. I slowly glanced around until I spotted a tall, burly figure lurking near the edge of the snow-covered evergreen forest. "Hey!" I yelled at them. "Did you see what made these tracks?"

When they turned and disappeared in the woods instead of answering, I abandoned every bit of my common sense and began to run after them. It was more like a swift plod through the ankle-deep snow. Time for a faster method of travel. Golden sparkles swirled around me as I, clothes and all, transformed into a sleek black panther. Holy crap, that's cold! I thought as my paws hit the snow. "For crying out loud, Shelly!" I heard Eddie's frustrated voice behind me. I got over it and soon was leaping through the wintery wonderland at a fairly quick pace.

That is until an arctic tern darted out from a nearby bush into my path. My feline brain got distracted from my mission. I lept straight up into the air and caught the bird with my paws. I didn't calculate the layer of ice under the snow in my landing, and I skittered around on my hind legs right into a nearby tree. The person disappeared into the forest out of my sight.

Eddie caught up. He took one look at me. "Bad kitty! What's in your paws?" he asked in a mock-stern voice.

I changed back to my vampire form. "Shut up," I said. The unharmed bird darted out of my hands and hovered out of reach just to give me an ironic obscene gesture before it flew skyward.

I realized that the tiny saddle on its back was completely empty.

A horrified thought rushed into my head: Did I accidentally hurt or even kill the rider? "Hello?" I called as I walked back to the bush. "Are you alright?"

"Uh, babe?" Eddie asked. "What are you doing?"

I pushed back the branches in a fruitless search effort. "I'm looking for that bird's rider."

"It had a rider?"

I nodded. "Yeah. I saw a saddle on the bird's back. Plus, someone obviously taught it how to give someone the finger."

He joined me in my search. "And here I just thought it was a super smart bird."

We searched with no luck for another few minutes before calling it quits. I had probably traumatized the rider so badly that they were never going to trust any vampire ever again. We headed back to the pub and went in through the front door. The place was still empty. Our disappointing meal still sat listlessly on the table. "Should we leave or wait for someone to come back?" I asked.

Eddie shrugged. "I don't know. But I am very curious how this place can run with only one employee."

"Who is most likely dead," I added.

He nodded. "I guess we should leave?" He pulled a twenty out of his wallet and left it on the table before we headed out the door.

"I think we should pick out some groceries before we go back to our room," I suggested. "Considering that O'Tannenbaum's is probably permanently closed."

Chapter Five:
A Little Noeledge is a Dangerous Thing

We left the pub in hopes someone would come along to lock up the place and trudged in the snow to Sargent Peppermint's General Store. The glowing sign of a cartoon peppermint candy wearing a drill sergeant's hat saluted the two large cats attached to a sleigh sitting outside the building. Images of flying silver owls decorated the sides of the pink sleigh. The spotted light brown lynxes stopped grooming themselves and purred at Eddie as he stopped to admire the sleigh.

"I have never seen one of these before," my husband said excitedly as he peered at the dashboard.

I looked at him in surprise. "You've never seen a sleigh

before?" One of the lynxes affectionately bumped its head into my leg and nearly knocked me over. I scratched the lynx's head.

The vampire pulled me over to admire the dashboard with him. "This is an all-terrain chariot." He pointed to a row of silver buttons, each labeled for a different kind of terrain: mountains, hills, plains, tundra, desert, swamp, forest, jungle, and plateau. "When you press one, the chariot automatically adapts for whatever you're driving over."

"So how come you've never built one?"
"Because they work best with animals pulling it. I like to be behind the wheel of something with mechanical power any day."

I looked at the lynxes and then at Eddie. "So, are you saying that this chariot is pulled by cat paw-er."

"Oh, good god," he groaned at my terrible pun.

"My jokes are hiss-terical. No claws for concern."

"I'd be lion' if that I didn't say that was a terrible joke."

"This is why you meow-rried me."

"Your puns are furmidable!"

"Aww, I'm tickled lynx."

Eddie frowned. "Really reached for that last pun, didn't

you?"

"Yep, that's it for meow." I shivered from the cold. "Are you done ogling at the all-terrain chariot so we can go inside?"

Eddie smiled. "If you insist, babe."

"I do, honey."

The inside of the store was a welcome relief to my shivering body. The ever-present aroma of peppermint tickled our noses as we took in the sights and sounds of Sargenent Peppermint's Store. Judging by the enormous section of various souvenirs slathered with their logos, it reminded me of one of those huge gas stations that doubled as a big box department store that took their love for their anthropomorphic peppermint candy mascot way too far.

Eddie held up a highlighter yellow one-piece swimsuit emblazoned with the little Sargeant Peppermint logo for me to see. "Hey, Shelly! I found your Christmas gift from me!"

I pretended to shield my eyes from the monstrosity they were calling a bathing suit. "Only if I get you the matching swim trunks!"

He laughed as he put back the swimsuit. "I'm good, thank you. I'm going to see what kind of groceries we can get here." He headed over to the food section.

I looked around until I spotted the sweatshirts. I made a beeline for them and smiled at what I saw. Each one looked like the love child of an ugly Christmas sweater and a hoodie. I picked out a purple one with the words: Jingling My Way to Sergeant Peppermint's. Below was an image of Sergeant Peppermint driving a bright red sleigh decorated with mini Christmas trees. A reindeer with brown wings was pulling the sleigh as the peppermint candy mascot was urging it on with a red and white striped whip. The sled's runners looked like a saluting candy cane version of the store mascot. Apparently, the company's marketing teams refused to consider the horrifying implication of Sergeant Peppermint using his fellow candies for parts of his sleigh. Still, it would make a great conversation piece. I took a few pictures of a few more equally terrifying hoodies before going off in search of my husband.

I found Eddie staring at two jars of jam in frustration. "Does this store sell any jam without peppermint in it?"

I glanced down at the red grocery cart he had snagged. Every food was stamped with Sargenent Peppermint's seal of approval with the words "a little bit peppermint in everything." Upon closer inspection, I realized the candy mascot was not kidding because the second or third top ingredient was peppermint. Peppermint bark candy. Delicious. Peppermint-flavored iced coffee drink. Great. Peppermint bagels. Good. Peppermint bread. Okay. Peppermint peanut butter. Interesting. Peppermint tortilla chips. Gross. Peppermint nacho cheese. Disgusting. This store had taken their love of peppermint to the extreme. "I don't think they sell anything without peppermint."

He let out a defeated sigh as he made his choice of the strawberry peppermint one and placed the grape jelly back on the shelf. "I think the only non-peppermint flavored food they sell here is the bottled water." He looked at my new find. "That's quite the interesting hoodie there."

"It's not just a hoodie. It's a conversation piece."

"In more ways than one."

"I think I saw a red one in your size. Do you want me to

grab it for you? We can be hoodie twins.”

“I think one ugly sweater hoodie will be fine for us.” He checked the price tag. “I see you’re keeping up with your 50-dollar sweatshirt souvenir tradition.”

“It’s 50 dollars of warmth, and that’s all that matters.”

“Can’t complain there,” Eddie replied as we wheeled the cart towards the only checkout lane.

In front of us was a tall elfin woman decked out in a heavy pink and white parka with brown fur trim around the hood with a pair of matching ski pants. She took off her black, warm-looking gloves to pay the cashier with her credit card. ‘How’ve you been, Brenda?”

The glum-looking sasquatch slumped her massive shoulders under the snug red and white striped polo shirt with matching khaki pants. A red barrette clipped back her honey-colored fur. “It’s been better,” she replied sadly as she finished stuffing the last of the elf’s supplies in a large pink backpack. She glanced over at Eddie and I with her dark brown eyes. Then as if an invisible hand turned a switch on her back, Brenda suddenly sat up, revealing her huge eight-foot-tall frame.

A huge smile spread across her face. "To tell you the truth, Freya, this has been the best year in Ho Hoboken! Present production has been up 1000%!"

The elf skeptically raised a blond eyebrow and was about to comment, but was interrupted by an excited, young voice.

"What treasure are you looking for, Freya?" Sitting behind Brenda on a stool was a much smaller sasquatch. Bits of her honey-colored fur stuck out from under the old school's aviator's cap complete with goggles she was wearing. A white scarf was wrapped around her neck and pulled together the rest of her Amelia Earheart outfit: a brown pilot's jacket with a white fleece lining and brown pants.

"Well, Bluebell, I'm looking for the lost scrolls of ancient Pedestria," Freya said with a huge grin.

The young sasquatch's brown eyes widened in awe. "Wow! That's awesome! I wish I could go treasure hunting with you"

"Maybe, when you're older," the elf suggested, "right now, you should focus on your treasure hunting club you started."

I looked over at Eddie. *I wish we were treasure hunting*

right now instead of being referees in this dumpster fire, I telepathically told my husband.

Then we wouldn't have this opportunity to save Christmas, he responded.

I prefer the idea of saving Christmas in a much warmer climate.

Multiple loud meows coming from outside diverted all of our attention. "I'm coming, Tonka and Pita!" she shouted as she grabbed her purchases and receipt before rushing out the door, waving goodbye.

Bluebell let out a disappointed sigh. "I wanted to show Freya my new clubhouse," she pouted.

Brenda patted her daughter's head. "Maybe next time, sweetheart." She turned her attention to us. "Welcome to Sergeant Peppermint's General Store. Did you find everything you needed?"

"I think so," I said as I slapped the hoodie onto the conveyor belt.

"Oh, you're actually buying that?" the young sasquatch said in a surprised voice.

"Bluebell!" her mother said a voice that amplified both admonishment and horror. "Apologize to her majesty."

At this point in our trip, I didn't even question how Brenda knew who I was. Santa or his minion, Clyde, probably sent pictures of Eddie and me to every resident of Ho Hoboken as a warning to be nice to the royals under penalty of death.

"Sorry," the kid said then mumbled under her breath, "that my mom's store only sells really ugly Christmas sweaters."

It was hard, but I managed to hide my smirk. Fortunately, her mother didn't hear her smart-alec remark. I liked this kid already but decided to quickly change the conversation so she wouldn't get in trouble. "That's a cool aviator hat!"

Bluebell grinned as she touched the goggles. "Thanks, it's my adventure hat! I'm the president, vice president, treasurer, and secretary of the Adventure Seekers Club. Our motto is: Look out, adventure! Here we come! We even have our own clubhouse and everything!"

"That sounds like a lot of fun," I said as I helped my husband unload the shopping cart. "I had a clubhouse when I was little."

"Was it a secret clubhouse? 'Cause mine is. It's a secret clubhouse. I found it."

I shook my head. "No, just a treehouse I shared with my older brother."

"My clubhouse is girls only. Boys have cooties."

"Fortunately, we outgrow our cooties," Eddie assured Bluebell.

The sasquatch gave an understanding nod. "Do you want to see my clubhouse, Your Majesty?" she asked.

Brenda quickly interrupted her daughter. "You know I don't want you to go beyond the factory."

"But, Mom," Bluebell protested

"Don't bother them, Bluebell. The queen and king probably have a lot to do and can't see your clubhouse."

"It's no trouble at all," I said. "We'd enjoy seeing her clubhouse."

"It's too dangerous for her," Brenda said.

Even though the young sasquatch had the build of a gorilla, I understood her mother's fear. "Another time," I told Bluebell. We paid for our groceries without further discussion of the clubhouse and went back to the hotel.

Eddie and I were putting away the perishables in our room's minifridge when we heard a knock on the door. When I looked through the peephole, I was surprised to see Bluebell out in the hallway. "What are you doing here?" I asked her.

She handed me a package of peppermint fudge. "You forgot this."

I looked at the fudge. I didn't remember seeing it in our cart. "Hey, Eddie, did you buy some peppermint fudge?"

My husband came over. "No," he said as he looked longingly at the fudge. "Did you?" he asked me hopefully.

I had a feeling I knew what the sasquatch was up to. "We didn't buy any fudge."

"Okay," the kid said. "Look, I need to show you my clubhouse because I saw Mr. Claude snooping around it this morning."

"Didn't your mother say you couldn't show us your clubhouse?" Eddie asked her.

"She changed her mind and said it was okay," she replied

rather quickly. "I don't like Mr. Claude, and I think he did something to our clubhouse. He yelled at me and Florence and said we were thieves!"

I didn't like Claude either, and the fact that he was sneaking around a kid's clubhouse had me concerned. "Do you have any idea why?"

"Hi, Bluebell!" Little Florence came running up to us with Pinkerton bounding behind her. "Have you shown the queen our clubhouse yet?"

Bluebell shook her head and turned to me. "Me and Florence found the clubhouse. So finders keepers. I don't know why a mean grownup, like Mr. Claude, would want a spaceship anyway."

That caught my attention. According to Eddie, aliens don't exist, but I wholeheartedly believe in them. "I'm intrigued," I said. The girls' faces lit up like a Christmas tree. "Awesome!" Bluebell said excitedly as she and the elf high-fived each other. "I'll give you the fudge for free if you'll let me show you my clubhouse."

Wow! She knew how to play every angle. "You drive a hard bargain, Bluebell," I said. "We have a deal." From the corner of my eye, I saw Eddie retrieve our weapons from our suitcase. I caught the red leather-bound book secured with a purple book strap he tossed to me and said the magical incantation, "Knowledge is Power." The girls watched in astonishment as magical green sparks swirled around the book as it turned into a deadly sixteen-inch silver sword with a red leather hilt in a matching red leather sheath.

"You've got a magical sword!" Florence exclaimed.

"Yep," I replied as I attached the book-strap-turned-sword-belt around my waist and secured the sword with the double leather loops on my left side. "Ready to go?" I asked Eddie as I put on my coat. Even though the coat covered my sword, it wouldn't be very practical in any kind of combat situation. I removed both the coat and sword belt. Fortunately, the belt could be adjusted to be worn in several different ways. I put back on my coat and converted my belt so Knowledge could be strapped across my back.

"Ready." Eddie's ensemble was easier. Vengeance was its club form with the scythe blade hidden from sight. My husband just stuck it into one of his coat's deep pockets.

As we followed the girls, I was amazed by how fast Bluebell moved. The young sasquatch seemed to glide effortlessly across the snow even with her elfin friend sitting on her shoulders. On the other hand, both Eddie and I clumped our way behind them. I now knew why there was never any evidence of sasquatches in the non-magical realm I came from. We followed the girls through a dark, snowy wooded area of gnarly tree roots. Twenty minutes later, Bluebell announced that we had arrived at the clubhouse as she set Florence down.

Eddie and I stared in amazement at their "clubhouse." It looked just like one of those round-flying saucers you see in old movies. Four metal legs held up the ship's body. I expected to see a green-skinned alien walking down the ramp, saying, "Take me to your leader." The snow-covered green and brown ramp was empty.

"Your clubhouse is an alien spaceship?" I asked.

"Pretty cool, huh?" Bluebell said as she and Florence raced up the ramp into the ship.

Pointing towards the spaceship I telepathically said to Eddie, If aliens didn't exist, then where did this come from? When he ignored me as he looked around, I took out my cell phone and began snapping pictures of the clubhouse.

"Come inside!" Florence yelled to us.

"Just a minute!" I answered as I started walking towards the ship. A rustle of branches off to my left caught my attention. I looked around but saw nothing. "Probably just a wild animal," I said to myself as Eddie and I walked up the ramp.

When we got inside, the first thing I noticed was the odor. The same faint strange rotten cucumber odor I had smelled both on Claude and Santa. The interior was a lot smaller than I realized. The room was about the size of an SUV. Three green, egg-shaped chairs with holes in the back sat in front of a panel that ran the length of the entire ship. There was only one large window facing the front of the ship. But the chart on my right caught my eye. Strange lettering ran up and down one half of the chart, and there were several images of moons and planets on the other side. Some of the planets were crossed out in red, and some had a huge green check mark on them. Our earth had nothing on. I took some pictures of the charts while Bluebell and Florence twirled around in the chairs.

"Do you recognize this writing?" I asked my husband

"Never seen it before," Eddie said. "We can ask Gunther tonight."

"Who's Gunther?" Florence asked.

"He works for the queen and me," Eddie explained. "Where did this thing come from?"

"Me and Florence were looking for mushrooms with my Uncle Eli and his dog, Goliath, when we saw it land," Bluebell told us. "We wanted to go see, but Uncle Eli told us to go back home." She paused sadly. "He never came back."

"I'm sorry," I said.

"He's not dead," Bluebell said.

"He's missing, like Mrs.Claus," Florence explained.

I just nodded but said nothing. Bluebell's uncle was probably dead like Mrs. Claus, but I didn't want to break these girls' hearts with my suspicions. Dealing with the loss of a loved one can be really hard on little kids.

I took some more pictures before a piercing, wailing siren

rang throughout the area. A giant digital clock appeared on one of the panels, and strange symbols began flashing on the screen. I recognized a countdown when I saw one.

"Everyone get out of here!" Eddie shouted above the alarm as I grabbed both of the girls' hands. We all raced down the ramp and began hightailing towards the woods. Glancing over my shoulder, I saw the spaceship start rocking violently back and forth. This was not going to end well. There would be no way we could make it to safety in time. I began looking around for some cover when my husband ordered everyone to get behind him.

We hurried behind the vampire as he held out both hands in front of him. He shouted, "Citadel!" A green force field immediately encapsulated us in a large bubble. A blinding white light flashed before us and was followed by a thunderous WHOMP which shook the area around us. Then the woods fell silent. Eddie waited a few moments before dismissing the protection spell. "I think we're safe," he said, surveying the area for any danger.

Holy crap!" I exclaimed as we stared at the scene before

us. What remained of the spaceship was a perfectly round scorched crater. The entire clubhouse had vaporized!

"Our clubhouse!" Florence moaned.

"It's gone!" Bluebell exclaimed. "Who would do this?"

They both looked to Eddie and me for an answer we didn't have.

<h1 style="text-align:center">Chapter Six</h1>

<h2 style="text-align:center">There's No Place Like Gnome for the Holidays</h2>

Both of the girls' mothers were waiting for us in the lobby when we got back to the Holly Jolly Inn. "Thank you so much for finding them, Your Majesties!" Brenda said.

I looked over at the young sasquatch. "I thought your mother said it was okay for you to show us your clubhouse," I asked her.

"Bluebell, I specifically told you not to go into the woods!" her mother exclaimed. "Do you want to end up missing like your uncle?"

The ten-year-old rolled her eyes. "Nothing happened to us, Mom."

"Don't you roll your eyes at me, young lady!" Brenda snapped.

Carol Ribbonhauser wrapped her arms around Florence.

"Florence Ribbonhauser, I told you to stay in the inn! You know how dangerous it is out there."

"But Mommy," the seven-year-old said innocently, "Queen Shelly and King Eddie protected us from the explosion."

"What explosion?" both mothers asked at the same time.

Eddie and I looked at each other as we mentally tried to come up with a believable story, but Brenda and Carol glared at us, seemingly daring us to tell a lie. I finally caved. "Their clubhouse exploded, but no one was hurt," I quickly explained.

"Narc," Bluebell said under her breath.

I don't know what horrified Brenda more: her daughter talking back to the queen or learning that her daughter's clubhouse had exploded. "Apologize to their Majesties!" she demanded of her daughter.

"It's all right," I said as I held up my hands to placate both mothers. "I'm sure she didn't mean anything by it."

A chilling breeze swept past as the doors to the lobby were flung open. Claude and Santa marched into the lobby. They took one look at Eddie and me and gasped before running out the door. We all shared a confused look. "What was that all about?" Brenda asked.

A look of horror crossed Carol's face. "You're going to report us to Santa!" she exclaimed as she threw a protective arm around her daughter.

This time, Eddie intervened. "No one's reporting anyone," he assured the innkeeper. "I think the queen and I weren't supposed to survive the explosion."

Both mothers gasped. "Santa wasn't always like this," Brenda said. "My brother, Eli, was a close confidant of both Mr. and Mrs Claus, and even in private, Santa was never like this until—-." She stopped talking and looked around nervously as if someone was listening to her every word. "Bluebell, we have to go back to the store," she grabbed her daughter's hand and left the hotel without another word.

"I have some paperwork to do. Have a good evening, Your Majesties," Carol said as she took her daughter's hand and led her away.

Eddie and I were left alone. "This place is getting weirder every minute," I said to him.

He nodded. "I just don't like the idea Santa and Claude

tried to kill us."

"Neither do I, but I need to get to the bottom of this mystery." I thought for a moment about how we would go about it when an idea came to me. "I wonder where Ho Hoboken's library is."

"It's about halfway towards the toy factory on the left next to the Sugar Plum Bakery," Eddie said, casually.

I stared in surprise at my husband. I normally pointed out libraries wherever we went. "When did you see that?"

"On our way to the toy factory."

"How could I have missed that?"

"Because you were too busy complaining about the cold to notice?" He surmised dryly.

"I'm a queen. I have every right to complain about the cold."

Eddie pretended to nod sagely. "Come, my chilly queen, and I shall guide you to the library," he said as he gave a deep bow and took my hand.

I rolled my eyes at his over-dramatic display. "Lead the way, drama king."

After another five minutes of tromping through the freezing cold, we found ourselves staring up at the engraved sign on the small stone building. "Ho Hoboken Library," I read aloud with a frown. "That's disappointing."

"Why?"

"I just thought they would have given it some kind of a Christmas pun." I pulled on the ice-covered metal handle of the glass door. Pointy little icicles rained down on our heads as the door slowly creaked open. Someone could lose an eye if they weren't careful.

The warm interior did nothing to offset the claustrophobic effect of the tiny, one-room building. Christmas-themed books leaned every which way and were haphazardly shelved back on the two bookcases. An ugly red and green plaid armchair that I swore belonged to every grandparent in history was centered in the middle of the room next to a round table from an earlier decade. A clipboard with barely legible names, book titles, and dates scribbled down on a legal pad was on the bright yellow Formica table top. Whoever was running this DIY library obviously never heard of patron privacy.

"Hey, Shell! Come take a look at this." While I was shaking my head in disgust at the lack of a properly run library, my husband was staring at the bulletin board hanging on the library's only empty wall.

I wandered over to join Eddie. Pictures of Christmas from years past cluttered the bulletin board. Even though the hairstyles, outfits, and most of the people changed throughout the years, each picture portrayed a scene of how merry and festive Ho Hoboken was usually. Tiny people with mouse-like ears and long, thin tails posed for various pictures under the Christmas tree in the Holly Jolly Inn. The Imaginavision Room apparently was the happening place to be for the holidays, sans the huge motor clog embedded in the wall.

Various pictures depicted the factory workers and the security guards joyfully gathered for their annual Christmas party. Both elves and sasquatches happily held up their full rum-infused eggnog glasses as they posed for the camera. There weren't any festive photographs of Ho Hoboken office parties this year to be seen anywhere on the bulletin board.

"Normally when a tragedy like Mrs. Claus' disappearance hits a town, I'm not surprised that the townspeople are feeling less festive than usual," I observed.

"I feel a 'but' coming," Eddie said.

I nodded. "But everybody here is acting as if either nothing ever happened or it's no big deal. I mean, the first Christmas after my mom died was hard, but my dad didn't make Robin or me act as if nothing had happened to our family, nor did he act like it was no big deal."

"How did you handle it?"

"All right. The three of us opened presents on Christmas morning, and then Dad hosted a Christmas lunch with the Millers, Andrew, Matt, Dusty, and Chris where we all exchanged gifts with each other."

"Timothy's been in the hospitality business long before owning a restaurant."

"He and my mom always enjoyed hosting events, and Dad wanted to continue the tradition."

"Growing up, my family never invited friends over for the holidays."

"That's kind of sad. Why?"

"Because who knows if your kids' friends were friendly with vampires?" Eddie said with a mocking laugh.

"Yikes!" Eddie grew up in a family of vampire-hunting Welkies and was even trained to be one. Fortunately, he realized how wrong and racist that thinking was when he was in college. Unfortunately, his mother had disowned him when he became a vampire. "Your parents were messed up."

He nodded. "They weren't too fond of our family gnome in the home either."

"What's a 'gnome in the home?'"

My husband looked at me in surprise and then realized how new I was to the fact that Santa is real. He pointed to the pictures of the tiny people. "Okay, every family with kids under eighteen years old, gets a gnome in their home. The gnome lives with the kids year-round and reports back to Santa with the letters of what presents they want."

"Kind of like the Elf on the Shelf concept?"

"Not quite. For one thing, they're actual gnomes. Another thing, they get to know the kid or kids and don't report on their behavior."

"I like that concept. Much better than forcing kids to be good, or they won't get presents."

"When I was little, I always asked Santa for toy models of the various cars and motorcycles I drew in my letters. A few of them I actually built later on in my life," he wistfully recalled.

I smiled at him and then frowned when I recalled the conversation with Santa's missing secretary. "Ms. Doodleysqueaks did mention that even the gnomes had vanished. I wonder if Santa did something to them."

"Or they could've gone into hiding."

"This whole situation is weird," I said.

"It's weirder than you think," said a tiny voice from behind us.

Eddie and I spun around and scanned the room to find a young gnome no bigger than a mouse sitting atop one of the bookcases. "Oh, crap!" she said the moment we saw her. She scrambled to her feet and sprinted across the bookcases, her mouse-like tail flailing about behind her as she skidded to a stop in her black ankle boots at the bookcase's edge. The tiny guitar slung over her back thumped against her black leather jacket which sent her toppling.

With a few quick steps, I caught the gnome in my hands. "Are you okay?" I asked her as I brought her up to my eye level. She narrowed her green and blue eyes at me. "You tried to eat me and my arctic tern, Bowie!"

I realized what she was referring to. "I'm so sorry. We're following someone, and I got distracted," I said. She brushed back her hot pink and electric blue punk rock undercut mohawk. "It's okay, I guess."

"You weren't hurt when I accidentally attacked you, were you?"

"No, except for this rip in my new jeans." Eddie and I looked at the various tears in her black jeans as we tried to guess which rip was not premade. "I'm sorry," I said as I set her down on the table.

"No worries. The rip makes them look cool," the gnome replied as she took the tiny guitar case off her back to inspect it for damage. "I'm Phoebe Enfield, lead singer of the famous Eggnog Nation!" She introduced herself with a rock and roll salute.

"Well, I'm Queen Shelly and this is King Eddie."

"Cool! I've never met royalty," Phoebe replied. "Rock on!"

I smiled. "Well, I've never met a famous punk rocker."

A sheepish grin spread over the gnome's face. "Well, my punk

rock band is not quite famous yet. I mean, me and my sister,

CeCe, have only ten views on our Vidcom channel, but this

might be our year with Christmas being canceled and all."

I gave her a suspicious look. "Why do you want Christmas

to be canceled?"

"'Cause I want to get out of Ho Hoboken. Everything we

do here is Christmas-related. Do you know how obnoxious that

is?

Constant Christmas all year long would drive me nuts,

too. "I see your point."

"It's even worse if you're a gnome here."

"Why's that?"

"It's the destiny of every single gnome once we turn

seventeen. Do you want to explore the world or become a

dentist? Nope, you're a gnome in the home for life. No other options." She sighed. "But you're here to fix Christmas right?"

"Don't sound so excited," Eddie remarked.

She put up her hands. "Look, I'm sorry that Mrs. Claus has gone missing, and I know I sound selfish."

"Just a little," I said.

"I just want to get out of this fricking cold town," Phoebe exclaimed.

"Have you mentioned your feelings to your parents?" I asked.

"Are you kidding?" she asked in typical teenage fashion. "My mothers don't listen to me. They just tell me what to do. Mum had me deliver a message to you two. She and Mom are kind of the leaders of the gnomes."

That's who wrote the cry for help that had been shoved under our door. "Well, that's what Eddie and I are here for. You mentioned that there are even more weird things going on here."

"Well, Mum did say I should tell you about the giant, fiery egg that fell from the sky," Phoebe said.

A flaming, giant egg? I looked at Eddie with curiosity. A giant egg could mean anything, especially from the perspective of a gnome. "How big are we talking about?" I asked.

"Twice the size of the king?" Phoebe guessed. "Oh, and it was engulfed in gray flames."

My husband's eyes widened in surprise but not at the size of the egg. "I've never heard of gray fire before," he remarked.

"It appeared right around the time Mrs. Claus disappeared. It landed near the locked-up Sled Shed," Phoebe explained. "I was taking Bowie out for a flight when we saw it falling from the sky. The egg broke once it hit the ground, and the sworm burrowed immediately into the ground."

"The what?" I asked.

The teenager was about to tell us when we heard the library door open. "Your Majesties, where are you?"

I recognized the cervitaur's voice. What was he doing here? Had he been following and listening to us all along? "Hide in here!" I whispered to Phoebe as I quickly scooped her and put her in my coat pocket. "Not a sound!"

"Oh, there, you are!" Claude said excitedly. "I see you are taking your tour of the town." His plastered-on smile didn't hide the disappointment in his voice.

I was caught off guard for only a moment as my brain went into overdrive to scrap together a plan. I hope this works, I thought. "This isn't our hotel room, Eddie!" I exclaimed as my husband stared at me as if I had just announced I was a flying purple elephant. Thank god, he quickly caught on. "It isn't?" He asked, feigning surprise and dumbness.

"I'm so sorry. The severe cold must have gotten to the king's brain, and he seriously thought this was the Holly Jolly Inn," I lied ever so smoothly to the cervitaur.

Claude stared at me like the proverbial deer in headlights. He blinked and shook his head a couple of times as if trying to clear his head but soon gave up the effort. "Of course?" The question had started as a statement but unexpectedly took a sharp turn.

I placed a hand on Eddie's shoulder. "Come along on, dear," I said patronizingly as I pretended to guide him out of the building. The dimwitted, yet persistent cervitaur started following us. Fortunately, he didn't notice Phoebe wriggling inside my coat pocket, but I didn't know how it would last. Not wanting to risk it, I racked my brain for a way to quickly rid ourselves of him. A not-so-great plan came to me but I was very desperate. I threw back my head and let out my loudest and shrillest black panther roar.

Claude and Eddie froze in their tracks and stared at me in complete surprise. "Is everything all right, Your Majesty?" the cervitaur asked hesitantly.

I smiled as if nothing had happened. "Of course!" I said right before I broke out into another roar.

The cervitaur's eyes darted from me to Eddie and then back to me again. He slowly began to back away. "I-I hear Santa calling," he said as he bowed nervously. "Pardon me!" He took two steps backward before fully turning around and running away from us in terror.

I turned to Eddie. "And scene," I said as I gave a theatrical bow.

Relieved that I hadn't gone off the deep end, my husband began clapping. "Fantastic performance, babe. Even I was fooled," he said.

"Thank you. This is why it's important to have parents in community theater."

A shrill whistle erupted from my pocket. An arctic tern dive bombed me from the roof of a nearby building as Phoebe started to climb out of my pocket. "What are you doing?" I asked the gnome.

She didn't answer me but jumped from my pocket to the back of the bird. She landed gracefully on the bird's saddle. "Up, up, Bowie!" she urged the bird as she snapped the tiny reins. Together they swiftly began to flee towards the safety of the forest at the edge of the town. "She knew I was acting, right?" I asked my husband.

"I dunno," Eddie said with a shrug.

Crap, I had scared her again. Time to make amends, again. "Hey, Phoebe! Wait up!" I yelled as I cupped my hands around my mouth.

The bird slowly turned back towards us. "What do you want?" the gnome asked.

"I'm sorry," I apologized. "I didn't mean to scare you, again. I was just acting to get Claude away from us."

"Okay," Phoebe said with a wary look in her eyes.

"You mentioned that this egg landed near the Sleigh

Shed. Could you show us it?"

"I guess so," Phoebe said as she deliberately steered her bird just out of my reach. "Come on."

Eddie and I followed her back behind the toy factory. "I thought you were going to take us to the Sled Shed," I said.

Phoebe rolled her eyes as she steered Bowie toward the side of the building. The bird smacked the wall with his feet, and the ground opened under our feet.

Twenty feet later, We landed with a thud on a cold dirt floor. "Ow!" I said as I refused to move until I got my wind back. I looked up at Phoebe and Bowie hovering over us. "You could've warned us."

"Consider it payback for scaring me," the teenager said.

She had me there.

Eddie groaned. "Where are we?"

"The underground tunnel to the Sled Shed," Phoebe explained. "Come on. I haven't got all day."

Good thing vampires are fast healers. Eddie and I slowly got to our feet, and we followed the gnome into a train-sized, dimly lit tunnel. We were only walking a few feet when Eddie immediately stopped in front of a large, metal door. "Shelly, look at this!" he said, excitedly as he read the sign on the door. "It's the Letter Room."

"What's a letter room?" I asked.

Phoebe rolled her eyes at me. "It's the room where all the kids' letters to Santa are stored."

"Can we go in?" Eddie asked.

The gnome shrugged. "You can try, but Ms. Doodleysqueaks always keeps it locked when she's not sorting the letters."

I looked up at the gnome in surprise. "She sorts letters? I thought she was Santa's press secretary."

The teen looked at me as if I were the dumbest adult she had ever met in her short life. "She is, and sorting letters is part of her job," Phoebe explained. "When Santa suddenly recalled all the gnomes four months early, Ms. Doodleysqueaks was just as surprised as everyone else."

I recalled my conversation with the press secretary in my office. "Was that around the time Mrs. Claus disappeared?" I asked.

"It happened right before. Both Mom and Mum knew something was wrong, especially after the accidents at the toy factory. That's why we gnomes are in hiding."

Eddie, who only had been half-listening to the conversation, turned the doorknob. "Get back!" he shouted as we all took a few steps to avoid being buried in an avalanche of unopened letters that spilled out the door.

Something bright and colorful poked out of the pile. I carefully moved away a few of the letters to reveal a foot shape wrapped in Christmas-wrapped paper. "What the frig?" I reluctantly tugged on my find and pulled out a human-shaped Christmas present.

"Maybe, it's a big doll," Phoebe unconvincingly suggested.

My husband and I looked at each other. With our track record, it probably wasn't a doll. "You want the honors?" I asked him.

Eddie quickly shook his head. "Nope. You found it, you opened it."

I decided to play the helpless queen card. "What if it's booby-trapped? You're my Guardian."

"Fine, we'll do it together," he said as he stepped closer. He took Vengeance from his utility belt and extended it to its full length. "Ready?"

"Phoebe, you shouldn't look at this," I warned the teen. She didn't need to see whatever horrors were under the wrapping paper.

Once I made certain the teen wasn't looking, Eddie and I slowly cut away the wrapping paper. A few moments later, two of us were staring down at the shriveled-up, mummified husk of Denise Doodleysqueaks. Not what any sane person would ask Santa for.

A horrified gasp told us the gnome had looked. I was about to suggest that she should turn away, but instead, Phoebe snapped at the bird's reigns. Bowie let out a squawk of surprise before darting back down the hallway. We tried to chase her, but both bird and gnome flew up the secret entrance,

I sighed. "We're not scoring any brownie points with her, are we?" I asked Eddie.

He shook his head. "She's been accidentally traumatized by us–you mainly–three times in one day, and I'm going to say no." My husband wisely took a few steps back as he spoke.

I gave him the evil eye. "Unhelpful." I looked up at the opening high above us. "I'm still going to speak with her mothers," I insisted as I prepared myself to jump.

"Uh, Shelly, "Eddie said as he placed a hand on my shoulder. "Unless you can now read everybody's minds, I'm pretty sure you have no idea where the gnomes are hiding."

"Good point," I said as we walked back to the letter room.

"Now what?" Eddie as we stared at the deflated corpse. "We probably should report this to the proper authorities."

"Considering the way Santa handled a dead body before, I don't think that would be a wise move."

"Yeah–." Brights and flashing lights down the hall caught the vampire's attention, and he went to investigate. "You coming, babe?"

Investigate strange lights or hang out with a dead body? Who did my husband think I was? "Of course!" I sprinted after him.

It didn't take us long to find the source of the lights. They were coming from a window a few feet above a tall steel door labeled Sled Shed. I expected Eddie to be jumping up and down with joy at discovering the door to the famous sleigh. Instead, he just stared at the padlock secured to the iron pull handles. "Do these images look familiar to you?"

I nodded as I snapped a picture of the weird padlock with my phone. "They're just like the symbols in Florence and Bluebell's clubhouse."

Eddie looked up and down at the entrance for a way in. "This is the most secure door I've ever seen. I can't find any cracks for my mist form to slip through."

"What about the window?"

A fanged grin crossed his face. "Perfect." He turned himself into a green mist and floated up to the window. To my surprise, he quickly changed back and secured himself to the wall. "Shelly, get up here! You have to see this!"

Now I can't turn into mist like my husband, but I, like all vampires, can climb and stick to walls like a spider. Eat your heart out, Peter Parker. I quickly crawled up the wall and joined Eddie at the window. "What the?"

We were mesmerized in puzzled amazement at the scene

below us. One moment we saw Santa's sleigh in its traditional red and gold paint job with golden runners, luxurious-looking red velvet seats, and enough cargo space to fit about six pieces of stacked luggage. The next moment, it quickly changed into a red and gold version of the spaceship that the little elf and sasquatch had claimed as their clubhouse. This sporadic shifting went on for several moments before stopping suddenly as if someone turned it off remotely. The sleigh or whatever it was had returned back into your standard Christmas sleigh.

"What was that?" I asked Eddie.

He stared at me in shock. "No idea."

We heard footsteps coming towards the door. We both scrambled to the ceiling before a green and brown lizard the size of a human walked upright to the door. *What is a lizard doing here?* I mentally asked the vampire. *There's no way he would survive in this weather.*

Eddie just shrugged. *Maybe he lives down here?*

Maybe. But why would he be dressed in full desert fatigues? The scent of rotten fruit wafted below us. Something about the lizard smelled awfully familiar, but I just couldn't place my finger on it.

The lizard spent a few minutes trying to open the padlock. When that didn't work, he took out what I thought was a green water gun from the hostler on his belt. He aimed it at the padlock and pulled the trigger. The energy blast was so loud and powerful that it nearly knocked Eddie and me down from the ceiling. To everyone's amazement, the padlock remained unharmed.

"Preshixit!" The lizard creature shouted in frustration before storming back the way he came.

Come on, Eddie. Let's see where he's going.

Okay, Shelly, but we need to keep a safe distance.

I gave the vampire a thumbs-up, and we followed the lizard creature back to the secret entrance. He jumped up, clearing the hole completely. Eddie and I waited a few moments before crawling up out of the hole.

My Guardian discreetly peeked out of the entrance. *Weird, I don't see him anywhere.*

What? Where did he go?

Eddie looked back at me. *I don't know. Stay here. I'm going to get a better look.* He left me in the tunnel for a few moments before poking his head back. "All clear," he said as he helped me out.

I looked around the deserted landscape around us. The only tracks around us belong to Eddie, myself, and deer tracks. I took a whiff of the air to see if I could pick up the lizard's scent, but I got nothing until somethings big and hairy came lumbering at us

"You two! On the ground now!" shouted who I now realized was one of two sasquatches in the same security outfits that Bartholomew wore. They aimed large pistols at Eddie and me. "Hands behind your head!"

My husband looked at me and mentally told me to listen to them as he slowly knelt in the snow. I nodded and followed suit. The security guards lumbered behind us and expertly and quickly handcuffed us. "You're under arrest!"

Chapter Seven:
Using a Get Out of Jail Free Christmas Card

"Well, this is different," I observed as Eddie and I sat on a bed attached to a painted brown cement wall. I stared up at the ceiling trimmed with white, fluffy crown molding that could've been easily mistaken for frosting.

"This isn't the first time we've been to jail," my husband reminded me.

"True, but did the last cell look like the inside of a gingerbread house?" I pointed to the orange pillow he was leaning against. "I mean that pillow even looks like a gumdrop."

"You're right. The bars of the last cell we were in were just plain old iron, not painted like a candy cane."

"It's probably the leftover paint from our hotel room."

"Hey, quit your yammering, you two," snapped one of the same sasquatch guards as he ruffled the pages of the newspaper labeled Ho Hoboken Herald. He was leaning back in an old vintage swivel chair with his big, hairy feet on the top of the desk. "Dumb tourists," he muttered to himself.

He didn't realize or didn't care that Eddie and I heard that last remark. I could've made a big deal out of jailing the queen and king of Peregrin, but with so many people here turning up dead, I decided against it.

The other black-furried sasquatch who arrested us walked up to his coworker's desk, sipping a large mug of sweet-smelling coffee. "Think Bartholomew will give us a promotion for our work here, Jed?"

Jed nodded. "Of course, he will, Abel. We can now prove the elves are definitely responsible for Mrs. Claus' disappearance! Other than not getting me a cup of gingerbread coffee, what did you do with their belongings?"

Abel just shrugged. "I just tossed them in the supply closet."

"We're doing a great job guarding Santa's Workshop!"

Eddie and I looked at each other and rolled our eyes. We were arrested by the Mayberry Police equivalent of Ho Hoboken.

This was going to be interesting.

The front door of the security building opened and lumbered in Ho Hoboken's head of Security. His big brown eyes widened in horror the moment he saw my husband and myself sitting on the jail's bed. "Your Majesties? What are you doing here?"

"Oh, just enjoying the scenery here," I said casually.

Bartholomew whirled around on his employees so fast I thought he would break something. "Why are Queen Shelly and King Eddie behind bars?" he roared at Jed and Abel.

"The elves sent these two spies to snoop around the factory!" Jed blurted out as he pointed at us.

I looked at Eddie with fake aghast. *How dare they accuse us of that? We don't need anyone to send us snooping, I* telepathically told him.

He nodded. *We do that very well on our own, thank you.*

Abel chimed in. "We called Toymacher to let him know."

As if on cue, the front door was thrown open, and in stomped Guy Toymacher. "Where do you get off accusing me of corporate espionage?" he shouted at the sasquatches, barely noticing Eddie and me.

"What makes you think I had anything to do with this, Guy?" Bartholomew yelled back.

Guy jerked his thumb over at the other two security guards. "Isn't that what you told dumb and dumber?"

"Why would I risk my life by throwing the queen and king of Peregrin in jail?"

The elf gasped as he finally looked in our direction and I gave him a friendly wave. "If Santa finds out about this, we're all dead," he said in a hushed voice.

"At least, that's something we can agree on," Bartholomew mumbled as he lumbered over to Eddie and me. He fumbled nervously with the keys as he unlocked the cell door. "Please forgive us, Your Majesties." The head of security gave us a deep, respectful bow before turning to his employees. I know that sasquatches aren't telepathic, but Bartholomew's glare followed by the immediate groveling from Jeb and Abel could've fooled me..

Eddie and I hopped off the bed. "All is forgiven," I assured the sasquatches. "Your employees just made an honest mistake."

"Then what were you two doing sneaking around the toy factory?" Abel demanded.

"Uh," I started to say as my mind wildly, yet desperately tried to come up with a little white lie. Finally, my conscience instructed me to tell the truth, at least a part of it. "Well, the king wanted to see the sleigh,"

"The location of Santa's sleigh is kept as a secret," Bartholomew said as he narrowed his eyes on me. "How do you know where it is?"

Eddie and I looked at each other with subtle panic, There was no way we would get Phoebe involved. I didn't want to completely shred what little trust the teenage gnome had in us. "Lucky guess?" Eddie answered.

All the sasquatches and the elf crossed their arms and stared, daring us to lie some more. *Come on, brain,* I chided myself, *think of a plan!* My brain refused to cooperate.

"And I wanted to take a look at that damaged Stocking Stuffer," my husband quickly added, coming to my rescue.

The elf looked at the vampire with curiosity. "You think you can fix it?" he asked.

Eddie nodded. "Of course! I know a thing or two about machines."

Bartholomew tapped his chin thoughtfully. "Maybe you can settle a disagreement," he said

"Sure, that's why the king and I are here," I said.

"Guy here is blaming my security team for what happened to the machine that day."

The elf crossed his arms and snorted. "Sure, blame the toymakers who haven't had any workplace accidents before then."

This quarrel between Guy and Bartholomew would get us nowhere fast. I held up my hands. "Hold it, both of you. Tell us what happened–"

"Sure," Bartholomew interrupted me. "Just as long you don't side with Guy here 'cause he won't tell ya the truth."

I blew out a sigh. "Tell us what happened–. " I repeated. Guy opened his mouth to say something, but I stopped him by holding up my index finger. "Without blaming each other," I finished. "Can you two do that?"

Both men looked down at the floor sheepishly. They nodded. "It had happened the evening before Mrs. Claus disappeared," Guy started to explain. "My crew and I were finishing up for the day. Mrs. Claus had come down to inspect the machines." He paused. "Now that I think about it, it was kind of odd."

"Why's that?" I asked.

"Mrs. Claus is the toy factory's bookkeeper. She would never inspect the machines."

I nodded. "Go on."

"She told us that she needed to find the serial numbers on the Stocking Stuffers for replacement parts. I assumed that Santa asked her to do it. My crew and I left her in the factory."

"I was working the night shift when I heard a loud explosion coming from the main floor. I went to investigate. The room was filled with smoke, and when it cleared, the Stocking Stuffer had a huge hole in it. One of the cogs must've malfunctioned and flew out of the machine. It's a good thing no one was in the Imaginavision Room when it happened 'cause that giant cog could have killed someone."

"Do you mind showing us the machine?" Eddie asked. Bartholomew and Guy both nodded and led us back to the toy factory.

The main floor of the factory was colder than it was earlier. I threw my coat hood over my shoulder and pulled it close around my face. I looked over at Eddie, Guy, and Bartholomew, all of whom seemed to have no issue with the indoor temperature. Even as a vampire, I'm still a wimp when it comes to the cold. I shoved my gloveless hands into my pockets to keep warm as we all stood in front of the damaged machine.

I decided to walk around the machine to keep my feet from getting frostbite. To my surprise, there was another poorly covered-up hole. At least they didn't slap a bow on it. I took a hand from my pocket and slowly peeled back the paper. This hole was about the size of a fist and its sharp, ragged edge was bent inwards. I squatted down to peer through the hole to get a better look. "Hi, honey!" I said as I saw my husband from the other side.

"Hey, babe," Eddie said with a startled look. He and the

others joined me. "Another hole?"

I nodded. "This was "This looks like someone punched a hole through the Stocking Stuffer and tried to cover it up."

"I didn't even know about this," Guy said.

"Neither did I," added Bartholomew.

Eddie crouched down beside me to get a better look.

"You're right, and it looks like there's something jammed inside."

I took out my phone and turned on the flashlight app to shine in the hole. Something shriveled cast an eerie silhouette in the light. Eddie started to reach his hand inside to grab the mystery object, but I quickly stopped him. "Don't reach your hand in there! It could still be on."

Eddie quickly drew his hand back because he knew I was right. "Good point. I prefer to keep both my hands." He looked at the elf and sasquatch. "Is the machine turned off?" he asked them.

"And unplugged?" I added.

"Yes," Guy responded.

"Here we go." Eddie cautiously reached into the hole.

After a few moments of twisting and turning, he finally pulled out

a shriveled, severed object "Here's one source of the problem."

"Is that a hand?" Guy asked, his eyes widened in shock

as his face turned green as if he was about to throw up. The elf

definitely wasn't used to seeing several body parts.

"More like a claw," Eddie said, taking a closer look at it.

"Anyone you know missing a hand?"

Bartholomew shook his head. "Nope." The gruesome

sight didn't seem to faze the sasquatch one bit. "What is going

on here?"

"It looks like you guys have a saboteur on your hands," I

said.

My husband intentionally ignored my awesome pun as he

set the hand down. He went over to extract the cog from the wall

in the Imaginavision room. "I can have your Stocking Stuffer up

and running in no time," he said. After asking both the elf and the

sasquatch for the tools he needed, he went right to work on the

repairs.

I watched the men work for a few moments before turning

my interest to the hand on the floor. The long curved claws on the thin hand intrigued me. It didn't look like any humanoid or sasquatch hand I had ever seen. I squatted down to get a closer look. "Are those scales?" I mused aloud.

All three men looked up from the repairs to stare at me in surprise. "What are you talking about?" Guy asked.

"It looks like scales are covering the hand," I explained.

Eddie stopped the repairs and joined me in my inspection. "You're right. It almost looks reptilian."

I almost missed the odd look exchanged between the elf and the sasquatch. It reminded me of the many times Eddie and I share a knowing secret just with a glance at each other. My curiosity started to overcome me, but I knew I had to be subtle about it. "Do you have security cameras here?"

Bartholomew glared at me suspiciously. "Why is that any of your concern?" he asked me.

"I would like to see your security footage of the incident, that's all," I quickly replied.

The sasquatch gave a reluctant sigh as he started up the staircase. "Come along, Your Majesty. I'll take you to the Aebersold Security Room."

I followed the lumbering head of security to a room right next to the conference room. A wall of television monitors greeted us when we opened the solid pine door. Bartholow sat down in the large, faded leather office chair and logged on to the desktop computer that sat on a long wooden desk stained with coffee cup rings. It took him a few moments to load up the footage of the explosion.

My mouth dropped in shock as I watched a white-haired elven woman wearing a green and red striped sweater with blue jeans and white tennis shoes leave a room and walk to the edge of the balcony. This was not how I pictured Mrs. Claus. A second security camera picked her up talking with Guy. Even though there was no sound, I could tell that something wasn't right with her. Her eyes kept darting around as if she didn't want anyone to know she was there. That made no sense. She was Santa's wife and probably could go anywhere she wanted to in Ho Hoboken. "Why does Mrs. Claus look so nervous talking with Guy?" I asked Bartholomew.

He furrowed his brow in thought at my observation. "I don't know."

This was not a normal activity for her. I nodded in response as I filed that bit of information away. I continued watching Mrs. Claus touch something near her left shoulder. The weirdest thing started to happen to her body. Her head started to blur and slinked its way down to her feet. Soon, all we could see was a blurry image of her. "Is something wrong with your equipment?" I asked the Sasquatch.

"What do you mean?" He replied.

I pointed to the distorted image. "Why is Mrs. Claus suddenly so blurry?"

He looked at me as if I had just grown a second head. "I'm sorry, Your Majesty, but I don't know what you're talking about. The picture is perfectly clear to me."

I looked at the screen and then back at Bartholomew. I was about to argue with the security guard, but he seemed so adamant about the camera's picture quality that I was starting to doubt my eyes. When I glanced back at the monitor, the image of Mrs. Claus was no longer blurry but now crystal clear with one gigantic difference. The elfin woman was no longer there, and a green and brown lizard-like creature wearing her clothes stood in her place.

Bartholomew wrinkled his brow in concern at the sudden change. "Odd. I don't recognize this person," he muttered to himself.

My jaw dropped in surprise. That was not the response I was expecting. Because elves are non-magical beings, they can't shape-shift. Normal people wouldn't have such a cavalier attitude when they witness an elf suddenly morph into a lizard creature. Maybe Mrs. Claus had some Welkie ancestry in her. "Does Mr. Claus normally do that?" I asked.

The sasquatch looked at me with a blank stare. "Do what?"

Did he not see the same thing I saw? "Shape-shift into a lizard!"

"I'm sorry, Your Majesty, but I don't know what you are talking about."

Was I going crazy within a year of my rule? Had this Christmas madness taken me, as well? I shook my head. I knew what I saw, even if Ho Hoboken's head of security didn't believe me. A clever idea to prove I hadn't imagined anything came to me. "Could you replay the clip?" I asked as I stealthily pulled out my cell phone. Once the sasquatch restarted the clip, I began to secretly record the scene so I could show Eddie.

I rewatched the scene leading up to the explosion. Mrs. Claus still transformed into a lizard creature, and Bartholomew still didn't seem to be too concerned about it all. The next scene showed the lizard going down the stairs to the factory floor. They walked around the undamaged Stocking Stuffer as if they were looking for some way to get inside. They got impatient within a few seconds and drove a clenched claw right through the running machine's metal side. The lizard soon realized their huge mistake and tried to pull their hand out, but it wouldn't budge. They yanked harder, and a basketball-sized gear went flying through the other side of the Stocking Stuffer, through the Imaginevison Room's plexiglass, and right into the wall. The camera's images violently shook as gray smoke billowed out from the machine. For the next few moments, static filled the TV monitors.

Bartholomew turned off the monitors. "That's everything, Your Majesty."

"Thank you, Bartholomew," I replied as I discreetly turned off the recording. "Wow! I've never seen anything like that before." Not a lie.

"Right after that, Mrs. Claus disappeared."

I nodded in fake understanding. In truth, I had even more questions than before. Was Mrs. Claus really the saboteur? Who or what is Mrs. Claus? What was up with Bartholomew? "This was very informative," I told the security guard. My brain raced as I tried to come up with an answer other than 'Holy crap! What did I just witness?' "I'll talk with the king to see what we can do to help," I replied with a good, safe, and ambiguous answer.

"Much obliged, Your Majesty," the Sasquatch said as he logged off of his computer. We walked back to where my husband was finishing up the repairs on the Stocking Stuffer. Bartholomew was impressed. "The king is done already?"

I nodded as I beamed with pride. "Yep, he's just that good!"

Eddie finished welding the cover to the second hole and lifted the welding helmet he was wearing. "Ready to plug her in?" he asked Guy as he stepped back to admire his work.

The toy foreman nodded as he plugged the Stocking Stuffer back in. The machine slowly roared to life. The elf stared at the vampire in amazement. "I didn't think this thing could be fixed," he said. "Thank you."

"You're welcome. This should put toymaking back in production."

"Let's hope so," Guy said.

"As long as Santa never finds out," Bartholomew interrupted.

Eddie and I looked at him in confusion. "Wouldn't he want the factory up and running?" I asked.

Both the elf and the sasquatch looked at each other nervously before Guy answered way too loudly, "As you know, things have been a little difficult around here, and we wouldn't want to upset Santa."

I was about to object but recalled the strange encounter of Santa yelling at non-existent employees. They had a good point of not angering the very volatile man in the red suit. "I understand," I said. The security video scene replayed in my head, and I was determined to get some real answers.

Obviously, not from Bartholomew or Guy. I decided to play my cards close to my chest. "If you no longer need our services, the king and I would like to take a stroll around your lovely town."

Eddie raised a skeptical eyebrow at me so high that it almost came off but said nothing. He was very curious to see what I was up to.

"It's rather chilly out, Your Majesty," Guy replied.

"It's not a problem," I said. "We vampires don't mind the cold."

My husband gave a bark of laughter but quickly turned it into a cough.

The elf was completely oblivious to the vampire as he rubbed the back of his neck. "All right, I'll show you out."

Once Guy left us outside to our own devices, Eddie looked at me. " 'We vampires don't mind the cold? Weren't you just complaining earlier about how cold you were?" he asked.

"I had a very good reason for stretching the rubber band of truth," I replied as I dug my phone out of my coat pocket. With my cold fingers, I opened up the video and showed it to him who watched with open-mouth shock.

"Oh, good! You see Mrs. Claus' image blurring out too," I told him. "I'm not the only one who saw it."

"Is there something wrong with their cameras?" Eddie asked as he replayed the clip to see if he missed something. "I don't know. Bartholomew acted as if the picture was pretty clear. He didn't seem to care about Mrs. Claus' blurring out, " I told him. "Do you think she might have some Welkie ancestry in her?"

Eddie shook his head. "Welkies' images don't blur out on camera when they shapeshift. I've never seen anything like this before."

"That's not the weirdest thing that happened. When she shapeshifted, Bartholomew wasn't even surprised."

My husband's mouth dropped open in shock. "Wait. What?"

I nodded as I shoved the phone back into my warm coat pocket. "He seemed to just shrug it off. He told me that he didn't recognize that person."

Eddie thought about it for a moment. "Maybe

Bartholomew is worried about insinuating that Mrs. Claus might be the saboteur and getting sacked by Santa," he replied.

"Or worst, getting killed by whatever the sworm is," I added. A shiver ran up my spine, and it wasn't just the cold temperatures. "Got any good ideas?" I finally said after a long silence.

"Going back to our hotel room and giving Gunther a call?" I smiled at my husband. "Now you're speaking my language."

Chapter Eight:
I'm Dreaming of a Weird Christmas

The door was ajar as we walked towards our suite. Eddie put his hand out to stop me from going in. With his free hand, he adjusted his war scythe, Vengeance, to its full, deadly length. "Stay here until I clear the room," he told me.

As I watched the vampire perform a security sweep of the room, I heard a very faint bubbling noise coming from all over the room. Did we leave the water running in the bathroom? "Eddie, do you hear that?"

He paused in his search to listen. He nodded. "I can't pinpoint where it's coming from."

I poked my head into the suite to help look around without my husband worrying about my safety. A blinking green light against the candy cane-striped wall caught the corner of my eye, and I looked up to see four small round objects adhered to each corner of the crown molding around the room. "Found it!"

Eddie carefully climbed up the wall like a spider to get a better look at one of the objects. "Gah!" he exclaimed in surprise.

"What's wrong?"

"It's an eye!"

"Eww. That's disturbing."

He reached out to touch it and quickly brought his hand back. "That's not the most disturbing part. It's an actual eye that seems still working." The vampire shuddered as he gathered up his courage to pull the sticky eye off the ceiling.

All four eyeballs suddenly detached themselves from the molding. I ducked as they flew into the hallway. I sprinted after them but a sudden blinding light flashed before me.

Eddie jumped off the wall and ran to me. "You okay, babe?"

I nodded as my eyes watered from the bright light. "Just give me a few seconds for my vision to return." I rubbed my eyes to hasten my vampire healing powers.

"The eyes must've vanished in that bright flash of light."

I squinted at my husband. "Magic?"

He shook her head. "Nope, but it's the same thing I sensed when we couldn't move from those chairs at the restaurant." He put a hand on my shoulder and led me back to our room which he now deemed safe.

Once the door was bolted shut, we took off our coats and draped them on a nearby chair. "Holy crap! It's freezing in here," I exclaimed as the icy air hit me hard. Getting my new ugly hoodie out of the shopping bag, I put it on and was amazed at how warm it was. "Good thing I bought this 'cause now I'm nice and cozy."

Eddie wisely didn't comment but steered the conversation back to the flying eyeballs. "I think those things were some sort of surveillance cameras."

"Great. This brings a whole new meaning to Santa seeing "you when you're sleeping.'" This entire trip had made a drastic turn from weird to downright creepy. I looked at the time on my phone. "We should get ready for our Zara call with Gunther."

Eddie took out his phone and said, "Maximum 10," as he waved a hand over it. The magic spell made the cellphone grow ten times its size. He did the same thing with his foldable phone stand and set up the phone sideways on it. After setting the phone and stand on the large TV stand, he called on Gunther on the video conferencing app before we both sat up against the headboard of our bed.

"Good evening, your Majesties! That's an interesting decorating choice." Gunther's face came into view when he answered. His eyes widened as he took in the gaudy wallpaper behind us. He and Dusty were sitting together on their living room couch.

"Hi, guys!" I said as I waved to them.

"That's quite the hotel room you got there," Dusty remarked.

"Yep, it's candy cane-themed. Delightful, isn't it?"

"Not what I was thinking," Dusty said. "More like: They need an interior decorator STAT!" He leaned in closer to the TV's camera. "Is that an ugly sweater you have on, Your Majesty?"

"Yes, it is, and it's quite warm," I said.

"Really," Dusty said. "Do they come in other colors, like pink or blue?"

"I think so."

The man smiled broadly. "Good. Could you get a large pink one and a large blue one?"

"Of course!" I said much to the satyr's dismay.

Gunther let out a sigh. "Please don't encourage him." He quickly changed the subject. "How is your meeting with Santa going?"

"'Jolly' is not the word I would use to describe Santa," I said.

"Really?"

"Yeah," I said. "Santa's a psychotic jerk. When we met him, he was completely wasted."

"Well, he's probably missing his wife," Gunther gently reminded us.

"Not with his shirt that read: Mrs. Claus puts the Ho in Ho Ho Ho," Eddie responded.

A shocked look came over both Gunther's and Dusty's faces. "Yikes!" Dusty exclaimed.

I nodded. "That was our reaction as well. But wait, it gets even better. When the head toymaker and the head of security were arguing, Santa wasn't even trying to calm them down."

"Wow!"

Eddie and I took turns telling the men about the events so far. "It's been weird, to say the least. Gunther, were you able to translate that message Eddie sent you?" I asked.

The satyr shook his head. "I'm afraid not. It's not one of the five languages I speak."

I frowned. "Okay, do you at least recognize the language?"

"I'm sorry, but I don't, Your Majesty."

I grabbed my phone and texted Gunther the pictures of the clubhouse/spaceship's interior and the padlock. "I just sent you pictures that might help."

Gunther studied the pictures. "What am I looking at?"

Eddie and I grimaced. Even the knowledgeable satyr was at a complete loss. "I think it might be the language written down," I said with uncertainty.

"I'm sorry, Your Majesties," Gunther apologized, "but I don't recognize the language."

"No worries," I said.

"What do you think is going on there in Ho Hoboken?" Dusty asked us.

I shrugged. "I don't know. It seems like everyone is on edge around Santa and his lackey, Claude. And there's a giant worm-thingy and the murders."

"What's next?" Gunther asked.

"I guess we'll do another round of negotiations and maybe investigate a little bit more tomorrow," I said.

"If we keep getting stonewalled, Shelly, we might have to call it quits," Eddie said.

"I know," I said with a nod. "I'd much rather spend Christmas in Peregrin with my family than in Ho Hoboken." I steered the conservation to a much more enjoyable topic. "Are you all moved in, Dusty?"

Dusty nodded. "Since I didn't have much stuff with me and most of it was already here, it was an easy move until your father roped me in to help him move that tree stand from his old restaurant into his and Amelia's house."

"Oh, thank God, I wasn't there," Eddie said with relief.

"I almost gave myself a hernia carrying that thing," Dusty

said. That thing is a three-inch thick piece of five-by-five plywood covered in a thin layer of red velvet which does nothing to protect your hands from getting impaled with splinters. Not only is the base awkward to carry, but the stand itself is made from twenty pounds of green Flexi-steel, a metal stronger than regular steel, but flexible enough to be shaped into any form. Believe me, carrying it is like lugging elephants around. "Timothy said normally you guys volunteer to help carry it."

"More like voluntold," I muttered. "I'm sure you helped out as well, Gunther."

The satyr smiled. "I was going to offer, but Amelia didn't want me to reinjure my hip and asked me not to help."

About six months ago, Gunther had fractured his left hip and leg when he went to confront on his own a dangerous portal devil Murad who had played a part in his late boyfriend's death. Little did Gunther know Murad had enslaved my father and his fellow police detectives from my hometown. It was Dusty who had saved the satyr's life and looked after him until Eddie and I came to their rescue.

"I didn't know your hip was bothering you," I said.

"Oh, it hasn't been," Gunther replied, "but your stepmother doesn't know that, and I didn't elaborate."

"Nice one, Gunther. Wish I had thought of that the last time Dad recruited me for lugging that thing."

The satyr smiled. "Your father did mention that he wanted to put it in the castle foyer, but I told him that you didn't need a second, massive Christmas tree."

"Thank you," I said with relief. We talked about a half hour more before my stomach began to remind me that Eddie and I hadn't eaten anything since our sub-par lunch at O'Tannebaum's.

Once we hung up, I retrieved the peanut butter, peppermint jelly, and bread from our mini-fridge and made two peanut butter and jelly sandwiches for ourselves as Eddie cast another spell to return his phone and portable phone stand back to their normal sizes. My tastebuds were assaulted with an overload of peppermint on the first bite and not in a good way.

"Minty," I said, grimacing. "Next time, we bring our food."

Eddie took one bite of his sandwich and quickly put it down. "Yep, we need to invest in some MREs. At least, our breath will be fresh."

I only ate half of my sandwich and then decided the intense peppermint was too much. An idea popped into my head. "I have a theory about what's happening here in Ho Hoboken."

Eddie washed down another bite of his sandwich with a swig of water. "What's that?" he asked.

"Aliens."

"Shelly, you know aliens don't exist."

"How can you be sure? I mean, we can't be the only ones in this universe. The club and the sleigh both looked like spaceships. Even people here called them UFOs."

"Technically, they're right." The moment he saw my surprised look, he added. "No one knows what the ships are or where they came from. Therefore, they are unidentified flying objects."

"Your unbelief is why the aliens haven't visited us yet," I remarked with a grin.

"Shelly, you're usually on the nose about these things, but trust me, aliens don't exist."

"All right, Scully."

"Does that make you Mulder?" Eddie said as he got up to turn on the electric fireplace.

I nodded with a yawn. "I don't know about you, but I'm beat," Eddie agreed. The day had worn us both out, and we needed a good night's rest. We both got ready for bed and crawled under the covers. Soon after kissing each other good night, I fell asleep next to my husband.

A massive lizard dressed in desert fatigues is pacing back and forth in front of a cold metal table. "If you tell me what the resistance's plans are, Nicholas, I will let you and your wife go," he demands.

Another lizard dressed like Santa Claus sits on the opposite side. His arms are restrained to the chair, and blood is running down his bruised, beaten face. He barely looks up as he speaks, "I don't know. I'm just a toymaker."

"Liar!" The lizard shouts as a spittle of red salvia flies from his mouth. "My troops know about the secret messages you have put in your toys!

"I have no idea what you're talking about, General Zigart,"

says Santa Lizard.

General Zigart slowly bends down and picks up a cane. He swings it across the table at Nicholas. The sound of wood striking across the lizard's face reverberates throughout the room.

The night sky lights up as spaceships fire upon each other. On the ground, Santa Lizard and a tan and blue leopard gecko with dark brown spots dressed like Mrs. Claus sprint across the ground to the safety of a dark alley. Santa Lizard quickly tosses aside a black tarp to reveal a red and green sleigh with golden runners.

They climb aboard, and Santa Lizard quickly presses various buttons and moves some switches. "Hang on, Doris!" he says as he pulls up on the steering wheel. The sleigh roars to life and lifts off the ground. With warp speed, it zooms up into the sky. Santa deftly dodges the incoming shots from the other spaceships before changing to warp speed and vanishing into the atmosphere.

I woke up with a start. "Bizzare," I mumbled. "That's the

last time I'm eating a peppermint-flavored peanut butter and strawberry mint jelly sandwich with peppermint-flavored bread." I looked over at my sleeping husband. Sometimes, my visions will awaken him, especially if they are really bad and horrific. This one was just weird, and I was sure it was just a weird dream with no need for analysis. I snuggled next to Eddie and soon fell into a dreamless sleep.

Chapter 9:
Claus Encounter of the Deadly Kind

Dull gray skies as snow flurries whipped around the drifts of snow outside our suite's window. A hot warm shower shook off the chill of the morning. As we got dressed, Eddie and I discussed our plans for the day. "I think we should keep our weapons on us in case this next meeting with Santa goes sour," my husband said.

I nodded. "Good idea. I definitely want to make it home for Christmas." I put on the belt holding my sword Knowledge in her red sheath and slipped my shield bracelet over my left hand. "We should put our bags in the egg beater in case we need to make a quick exit."

"My thoughts, exactly, babe," Eddie agreed as he clipped his war scythe in her compact form to his belt. He, too, slipped on his shield bracelet, just in case.

I popped two bagels into the suite's toast oven as Eddie packed our bags. "Mmm, more minty grossness," I said sarcastically.

"Just be glad I didn't get a dozen peppermint-flavored eggs."

"How is that–Never mind, I don't want to know."

"Me neither. I'm curious to see Santa's reaction when he finds out that the damaged Stocking Stuffer is up and running."

"Probably not a good one." I handed him my folded-up hoodie to pack it in his backpack.

"What's this for?" he asked.

"In case I get cold during the meeting," I told him. The toaster buzzed, and I took out our bagels and spread peanut butter on them. I took out two of the iced coffee drinks (peppermint-flavored, of course) from the refrigerator, and we sat down for another extra-minty meal. I told him about my weird dream from the night before.

"That has to be a side effect of too much peppermint," Eddie said. "I'm also pretty sure our conversation last night played a huge part."

I nodded as I finished my iced coffee and went to get myself a bottle of fruit dragon blood. "That's what I figured," I said. "We need to stop by Sargentant Peppermint's to get some stocking stuffers. I think it'd be great to see if they have mini jars of their peppermint-flavored peanut butter. We can give to everyone we know."

"Generously evil. I like it," Eddie said with a grin.

I laughed as the fruit dragon blood nearly went up my nose. Fortunately, none of my drink spilled on my shirt. We finished up our refreshing breakfast and headed out to the toy factory for another unproductive meeting with Santa.

The sound of our feet crunching in the fresh morning snow echoed loudly through the silent street. I pulled my hat over my ears to ward off the icy wind whipping around us. "Holy crap! It's even colder than it was yesterday!" I said.

Eddie nodded in agreement as he turned up the collar of his coat. "I'm even getting a bit chilly," he said.

"Hopefully it'll be warmer once we get inside the factory," I mused as we arrived at the back of the toy factory. I bravely removed my hand from the warmth of my coat pocket and began to push open the door, but nothing happened. The door didn't budge. "Maybe it's locked?" I suggested. I pulled on the door handle, but nothing happened.

Eddie noticed my raised fist hovering over the door. "Let's wait a few minutes before pounding on the door. They could be running late," he suggested.

I let my hand retreat into my warm pockets. "I just hope we won't freeze to death before they get here."

"I'm pretty sure no vampire has ever died of hypothermia."

"We'll go down in history as the first ones."

"How did you ever survive growing up in a cold weather climate?"

"I stayed inside as a smart person should."

"No sledding or building a snowman with Robin?"

"When I was young and foolish maybe, but he never missed any opportunity to chuck a snowball or two at me."

"Ah, brothers!"

"One winter, Dad and Mom took us cross-country skiing."

"Let me guess, you hated it."

"Yep," I said as I moved around to keep my blood circulating. "I almost became a popsicle."

"The cold never really bothered me growing up. Of course, the best thing was slugging Dirk with an energized snowball."

"Packed with a bit of ice?"

"Of course, but with brotherly love," he said with an evil grin.

We listened closely for any sign of life coming from the factory but were greeted with an eerie silence. Eddie checked the time on his phone. "Santa did say the meeting was at nine, right?"

I nodded. "Maybe they forgot," I said as I knocked loudly with my fist. "Hello? Santa? Guy? Claude?" I shouted.

No one answered me. I pressed my ear against the door as close as I could without getting my ear stuck to the icy steel exterior. I closed my eyes so I could fully concentrate on my vampiric hearing without any distractions. I was met with a stone-cold (pardon the terrible pun) silence.

"Anything?" Eddie asked.

"Nothing."

"Let me try something." The vampire quickly changed into a green mist and tried to dart between the cracks of the door. He barely got an inch through when he was violently propelled backward. He quickly changed back to normal but not before he landed in a snow drift behind us. "Wow! I wasn't expecting that!" he said as he scrambled to his feet.

I gasped the moment I saw him. "Are you okay?"

"I'm fine, babe," he said as he looked at the singed corner of his sleeve. "Good thing I was wearing my coat, and my backpack cushioned my fall."

"What happened? Did you hit a magical barrier?"

He shook his head. "I hit some kind of barrier but it wasn't magic."

"What do you mean?"

"Magical barriers don't burn objects. Instead, they just repel outside influences."

"If it's not magic, then what are we dealing with?"

"Don't know." He looked around for another way in but decided against getting burnt again. "I could try to pick open the lock."

"Let's not commit a felony," I said as I blew on my hands to keep warm.

"And break our record?" Eddie said with a grin.

"I just want to be responsible for a change."

My husband checked the time on his phone. "It's been almost fifteen minutes past nine. I say we head back to the–"

I barely let him finish his sentence before I broke into a run toward the warmth of the Holly Jolly Inn. As I neared the Egg Beater, I saw Santa's right-hand man slink out from under the helicopter. "Hey, Claude!" I shouted at the cervitaur. For a brief moment, his images flickered, and in his place stood a lizard dressed exactly like him before going back to the cervitaur. He sprinted off in the opposite direction. *Weird,* I thought, *he probably ran off to remind Santa about—.*

My thoughts were interrupted by a bright flash of light. I was blown back by what I thought was just the blast wave. "Why are there pieces of the helicopter everywhere?" I mumbled to myself, still trying to comprehend what just happened. Fighting the ringing in my ears and the disorientation in my head, I slowly realized just how lucky I hadn't been injured in the explosion.

My luck immediately changed as soon I heard the clanging of a bell right before I felt the tremors beneath me. A terrifying creature about the length of a school bus broke free from the frozen ground a few feet in front of me. Its head was as big as a great white shark and barred row after row of jagged dark stained teeth as salvia spewed from its oval-shaped mouth. Even though it seemed to have no eyes, the creature turned its white worm-like body toward me. Suddenly it lunged at me and sank its jaws into my leg.

The sound of bones splintering didn't even match the scream of pain escaping from my lips. As I collapsed to the ground, a horrifying realization swept over me. Not only was the worm snake thing latched onto my leg, but the creature began to drag me back down the hole it had emerged from. Before I disappeared into the ground, I saw the panicked-stricken face of my husband as he raced towards me. "Eddie!"

Even though I was in tremendous pain, I instinctively

tucked my chin down and wrapped my arms around my head. At least my coat was protecting my arms as my body thrashed around the tunnel's wall. Finally, the creature lunged into a huge underground cavern lit by thousands of colorful luminescent objects on the ceiling's stalactites. The smell of rotten flesh lifted off the bodies of the worm snake's victims. It flung me on the cold dirt floor.

Survival instincts overtook my severe pain. I scanned the room for an escape route. My only option was an entrance on the other side of the cavern. When the thing wasn't looking, I struggled to stand up, but my leg crumpled beneath me. There was no way I could run and make it out alive. Maybe I could crawl.

The creature lunged at me. For a brief moment, I thought it was the end until a green mist flew in front of me. "Citadel!" Eddie shouted as he materialized in front of me. The creature slammed into the ball-shaped green force field, but the vampire kept it intact as he picked me up, not realizing just how bad my injury was, and ran to the exit.

The worm snake chased after us, but my husband was

faster and smarter. Eddie made a sharp turn into a smaller cavern with no other exits. After he set me down on the cool dirt floor that made me whimper in pain, he faced the entrance and dissipated the force field before shouting, "Contengo!" as he conjured up another spell.

For a split second, it was deadly quiet. Then the walls around us shook as the worm snake struck the ward spell's invisible barrier across the cavern entrance. For a few long, terrifying minutes, the creature kept ramming into the barrier. Stalagmites began to fall from the ceiling, creating a colorful dust storm. Eddie crouched down beside me as he activated his force field spell around us. Snow and rocks rained upon the force field but the spell didn't waver.

The worm snake gave up and backed away into the darkness. Eddie dismantled his force field and saw the terrified look in my eyes. "It's over," the vampire said as he wrapped his arms around me.

The terror and shock slowly slipped away from me and were replaced by the excruciating pain in my injured leg. The moment my husband tried to move me, I screamed in agony.

Eddie was now registering the fact that my leg was bloody, bruised, and bent in a very unnatural way. "Just give it a minute to heal," he advised as he took my hand. "Breathe."

I squeezed my eyes shut and concentrated on my vampiric healing abilities. Kittens and rainbows. Kittens and rainbows, I repeated the mantra as I waited for my broken leg to repair itself. Nothing happened. "Come on! Heal!" I told myself. Still nothing.

"Let's take a look at your leg," Eddie said in a failing attempt to mask the sudden fear in his voice. He took off his backpack and pulled out a first aid kit and a switchblade knife. He flicked the blade open and carefully cut off my bloodied and ripped pant leg at the knee. He gasped loudly in shock.

"It's bad, isn't it?" I asked as I hesitantly opened my eyes. I immediately regretted my mistake and squeezed them shut again, but the image was already burned in my mind. Two pieces of broken bone were slightly jutting from my bleeding leg, but it still hurt like hell. That wasn't the most concerning thing about my condition. A yellow-green discharge oozed from the creature's bite marks. "What the frig is that?"

"I don't know, babe," Eddie replied as he began to attend to my wounds. "I think it could've come from that snake worm creature."

The moment the antiseptic wipe touched my injury, I let out a scream of pain as my skin began to sizzle. "Stop! My leg is burning!"

Eddie immediately held up his hands. "Your healing abilities aren't working, are they?"

I shook my head. "No, I don't know what's going on with them."

"Maybe you need blood." He rolled up his coat sleeve and prepared to cut one of his arm's veins with his fangs for me. "Here, I'll give you some of mine."

Images of the human blood-drinking assassin who had turned me into a vampire and his yellow red-flecked eyes rushed through my mind. Vampires like him who only drink people's blood will become very unstable and dangerous. Many of them have gone rogue and will kill and drain people without a second thought. If a vampire drinks a person's blood, that person is paralyzed and can not escape. I am not willing to cross that incredible unethical line to save myself. "No," I told him.

He nodded and then he remembered his hemotose pills. He dug the bottle out of his pants pockets and handed me a few of them. "Take these instead."

"Are you sure? I don't want to–"

"Shelly, I've lived without drinking blood for over sixty years, and a few days more won't kill me."

I swallowed down the pills and waited for them to start working. A few fruitless moments passed as I started to shiver uncontrollably. "They're not working."

Eddie touched my forehead. "You're getting a little clammy. I think you might be going into shock. Let's get your leg cleaned and immobilized and get you warmed up."
I nodded. I steeled myself and didn't scream in pain as much as I did earlier while Eddie did his best to quickly and efficiently clean and dress my wounds.

"It's over, right?" I hopefully asked right before I saw the vampire pull out my $50 sweatshirt out of the backpack. "What are you doing with my sweatshirt?" Most likely at this point, I started to suffer from delirium.

"It's the only thing thick enough to sufficiently pad your leg," Eddie explained as he flattened out the shirt and gently placed it under my leg. Then he pulled out two wooden stakes from the backpack. The vampire waved his hand over the weapons he had used back in his secret agent days as he said, "Maximum 10." The stakes magically doubled in their length three feet long, and he inserted them inside my wonderful shirt, one on each side of the torso portion. After wrapping them around my leg, he used the sleeves and his belt to secure the makeshift splint. "How's that feel?"

"A little better, but I'm still really cold."

He unfolded an emergency thermal blanket and wrapped it around me. "I think that creature's venom is somehow preventing your healing powers

I nodded as I gazed upwards. "Yep, I think you're –Hey, the ceiling looks like the sky's all sparkly."

Eddie opened his mouth to say something sarcastic in reply but when he looked up, he saw what I was talking about. The cave-in had caused a hole in the ceiling. He took out his cell phone to attempt to get a signal. "Zamnit!" he said. "I can't get any service on my phone."

"Throw up one of your energy spells to let people know we need help."

"And give our position away to Santa and Claude? I don't think so," Eddie said with a grin as he tucked his backpack under my leg to elevate it." Your injury must be more severe than I thought."

I was too weak to even roll my eyes. "Hilarious, dear," I muttered as I shut my eyes to ward off another wave of pain. I knew now just how much pain Gunther must have been in when he fractured his hip and leg.

Eddie sat down next to me with his back to the cave wall. "You should get some rest, Shelly," he said. He helped me rest my head in his lap. "It might help you heal." He paused as he remembered something. "Your sword is inside my backpack," he told me, knowing that would help me calm down

My husband was right. I shut my eyes and slowly drifted off into a restless sleep. Sometime later, I became vaguely aware of scuffling, unknown voices, and a dog barking all around me. I was too exhausted and in too much pain to do anything about it. The one thing I was absolutely sure about was Eddie's

determination to keep me safe.

Chapter 10:
Will the Real Santa Claus Please Stand Up?

Something wet dripped on my face and instantly awoke me. I opened my eyes to see a gigantic dog hovering over me. Slobber dripped from its big, pink tongue as it panted excitedly. "Gah!" I said as I managed to sit up on what I now realized was a brown and red plaid couch in a large cabin. The huge navy blue fleece blanket that had been covering me fell to the pine flooring. At first, I thought the brown and white floppy-eared pup was huge from my perspective on the couch. Now I realized just how big it was as I stared up into the eyes of a Brittney dog the size of a polar bear.

"Don't worry about Goliath, your Majesty," said a deep, gravelly voice coming from the other side of the cabin. "He won't hurt you. He just wants a scratch or two." The voice belonged to a nine-foot-tall sasquatch with dark brown fur who was grinding some kind of greenish-brown paste in a large marble pedestal atop a wide wooden bar table. He wore a red and black plaid shirt that was rolled up past his elbows under a pair of denim overalls.

My husband set down the coffee mug he was drinking from on the counter and hopped down from the barstool. He came over and kissed me. "Glad to see you up, babe," he said. "How are you feeling?"

"A lot better," I replied as I glanced down at my injured leg. Someone had rebandaged, re-splinted, and slathered it with a greenish-brown paste that smelled like someone had soaked gym socks in fermented juice. I ignored the foul smell and was delighted to see that my broken bones were no longer protruding from my leg. I bravely wiggled my toes with very little pain. "My healing powers seemed to come back, slowly"

Eddie nodded. "Then the ointment must be working. Want some coffee?"

I nodded. I scratched the giant dog between his ears as

his tail thumped happily on the floor. "Where are we?" I asked hesitantly.

"You and the king are in my cabin," the sasquatch replied as he finished grinding the paste and placed it in an enormous refrigerator. He then poured some steaming coffee into a normal-sized mug and gave it to the waiting vampire who added honey and a splash of milk for me. He walked into the living room and held out a hand the size of a hubcap. "Name's Eli. Goliath and I found and brought you here. Seeing that you were in pretty rough shape and all."

I shook his hand the best I could. "Thank you, Eli," I told him. Eddie handed me the coffee, and I inhaled the sweet aroma of lavender and honey. I took a slow, indulgent sip. "Wow! This is really good!"

Eli sat down in a giant navy blue armchair with Goliath at his bare feet. "Thank you. The lavender is from my garden."

I frowned in confusion. Wasn't Ho Hoboken a land of perpetual winter or did my online researching skills fail me? "How can you have a garden in this climate?" I asked.

Eli smiled at me. "I have a rather large greenhouse not too

far from here where I maintain a vegetable and herb garden, as well as a variety of fruit trees."

I nodded as I sipped my coffee. That made sense, but I wasn't going to admit it to anyone. I quickly changed the subject. "What is that stuff you put on my leg?"

"An antidote for the sworm's deadly venom. Ground mushrooms, fermented vinegar, and aloe. Something earthly can heal a bite from an alien creature, amazing isn't it?" the sasquatch said.

Eddie nearly choked on his coffee in shock. "I'm sorry, but did you say 'alien' as in outer space?"

Eli nodded as he raised a bushy eyebrow at him. "Yes, sire. Where else would it come from?"

"Uh, here on earth?" I suggested.

The sasquatch let out a hearty laugh that shook the walls. Then he realized we weren't sharing in his merriment. "You don't know, do you?"

Eddie and I shared a puzzled look before vigorously shaking our heads. *Did I miss something while I was out?* I telepathically asked my husband.

You got me, Eddie replied with a shrug. *I have no idea what he's talking about.*

A knock on the front door of the cabin interrupted us and caused Goliath to lift his head. The giant dog got up and began to bark excitedly at whoever was outside. Eli followed him and peered out the frost-covered window at the top of the pine wood door. He grabbed Goliath's collar and pulled him back as he let his visitor inside.

A short elfin woman stepped across the threshold. She stomped the snow off her thick black boots and unwrapped a thick rainbow-colored scarf from around her neck. When she threw back the fur-lined hood of her coat, she revealed a head of short, curly white hair. "Thank you, Eli," she said as she handed him her black peacoat to hang on a row of hooks near the door. Underneath her coat, she wore a simple red and green sweater with embroidered cookies and a pair of jeans. She wiped the fog off her gold-rimmed glasses, revealing bright green eyes. "You're up, your Majesty," she asked me. "How are you feeling?"

"A lot better," I replied hesitantly. Who was this woman who looked suspiciously like a modern-day version of Santa's wife? "Thank you—." I paused hoping the next words wouldn't make me look like a complete idiot if I guessed wrong. "Mrs. Claus?"

She gave me a warm smile. "The children call me, Mrs. Claus. You can call me Doris," she said.

"Aren't you supposed to be missing?" Eddie asked the important question instead of me.

"Well, that's what Nick and I agreed on until you and the queen showed up here and started poking around," she said.

That's what we do best, I telepathically said to Eddie who responded with a subtle grin. "Well, your secretary came to me and requested our help, Doris," I pointed out.

"We didn't expect that," she said with a sigh.

The front door opened again, and Santa in his classic red suit stepped across the threshold. I quickly reached into the backpack to pull out Knowledge to defend myself against the elf. The second my fingers touched the butterknife-sized sword, I realized that my husband had failed to reverse his shrinking spell.

At least, Eddie was better prepared to arm himself. The

vampire stepped in front of me as he drew his war scythe. With a press of a button on the handle and a couple of shakes, Vengeance lengthed to its full deadly six-foot length. "Don't even think about taking another step!" he warned.

Eli, Doris, and Santa looked absolutely horrified. "What are you doing, your Majesty?"

"Stopping you!"

"Why?" shouted the visibly confused Santa.

"I know you ordered Claude to blow up our helicopter, and I saw you summon that worm creature with that whistle."

Santa's eyes darkened. "Damien," he said in a not-jolly voice.

Doris unexpectedly reached into her pants pocket and pulled out a candy cane. With one flick of her wrist, the end of the candy lengthened to another twelve inches with an incredibly sharp point. She quickly stepped between Santa and Eddie. "Back away from him!" she warned the vampire.

"They don't know," Eli told Santa and Doris.

Santa nodded. He looked at his wife who lowered her weapon but didn't put it away. "Don't be alarmed with what will happen next," he said as he and Doris touched their left shoulders

My eyes grew huge with concern. "What do you mean by–What the?" I stopped mid-sentence and looked on in shock as Eddie and I witnessed the Claus couple turn blurry, starting with their heads and moving quickly down their bodies. After a few seconds of blurriness, they became clear, and in their place stood a red and green Caiman lizard wearing the same clothing as Santa and a brown and blue spotted gecko who also wore Doris' clothing.

"This is our true form," Santa explained. "Doris and I aren't from here. To tell you the truth, we're not even from this galaxy. We are from the planet Komodon in the Draconis Galaxy."

My mouth fumbled for words as my brain tried to wrap around what Santa had just told me. My mind raced through the names of known planets and galaxies, and neither name showed up on that list. I was pretty sure the man in the red suit would never tell a lie. That could only mean one thing. "You're aliens?" I finally managed to blurt out.

They both nodded.

Not only was Eddie just as shocked as I was, but he was also regretting the fact I was right about aliens existing. "How is that even possible?"

"Well, it's a long story," Santa replied. So Santa and Mrs. Claus began their tale.

Many years ago, a pandemic spread throughout the planet Komodon, killing over half of its shape-shifting, humanoid lizard population. As a result, their monarchy fell into disarray, and the ruling elite took control. For the first few years, everything went smoothly with the millionaires in charge. Doris was employed by one of the senators as his bodyguard when she first married Nicolas. Things took a turn for the worse when they were overthrown via a coup led by General Ziggurat. This brutal Komodo dragon man ruled Komodon with an iron fist.

About three years into his reign, a small but determined underground resistance group was formed. Nicholas was a toy maker. Doris approached him about joining the group. Nicholas was hesitant at first as he was a pacifist and didn't want to participate in any war, he soon realized that he could send secret messages to the other members hidden inside the toys he made.

Unfortunately, there was a mole among them. General Ziggurat captured and interrogated through torture both Nicholas and Doris in a failed attempt to discover who else was a member of the resistance. What no one could have anticipated was an attack from another alien planet. The surprise bombing allowed the Clauses to escape to Nicholas' spaceship which General Zigart's men had confiscated to search for secret messages.

Six thousand of our earth years ago, they arrived here in Ho Hoboken when their ship had run out of fuel. At the time, small tribes of elves, gnomes, and sasquatches lived there. Doris and Nicholas laid low for some time and shapeshifted into elvin forms. Eventually, Nicholas noticed how the children didn't have any toys to play with. He began building wooden toys and secretly leaving them at the entrances of the huts.

One Christmas Eve, an elfin child caught him in his lizard form leaving a wooden spinning top. Rumors of a lizard man leaving presents for the children spread through the tribes like heat from a fireplace. Nicholas and Doris came out of hiding and showed their true form to the natives. Soon both Nicholas and

Doris adopted the idea of turning themselves into Santa and Mrs. Claus. They started the town of Ho Hoboken and employed all of the elves, sasquatches, and gnomes who lived there.

"Damien the Hunter and his lackey, Claude, arrived right before the sworm landed here," Santa explained to us. "Eli and I saw his ship land here in the forest."

"How did they know that you were here?" I asked.

"We don't know," Doris said, "but I suspect a member of the Kaggen army must have seen us and informed them."

"Is that the other alien planet who attacked your planet?" Eddie asked.

Both Santa and Doris nodded. "We decided to go back into hiding with only Eli knowing our whereabouts," explained Santa. "Especially after the sworm bit him, we had to keep Damien from hunting us as Komondons know how to make an earthly form of anti-venom."

Eddie remembered his secret recording of Damien and Claude and the mysterious blob. He explained the situation to the Claus' "Can you translate this conversation for the queen and me?" he asked as he took his phone from his pants pocket and played the recording for them.

As Nick and Doris listened, a worried look spread across their faces. "They were using a communication device called a pheraphone to speak with General Ziggurat," Nick explained. "Apparently, there were complications in their search for Doris and me"

"Eddie and I are most likely the complications," I surmised.

"Sounds like it," Doris said. "The general told to Damien and Claude to take care of you, and report back to him when they have caught us."

"So what now?" I asked.

The Clauses shrugged helplessly. "I wish I could take your Majesties back to Peregrin," Santa said, "but Damien has the door to the sleigh ship under surveillance with the sworm constantly patrolling the town underground."

Eddie and I looked at each other. The Egg Beater had been scattered all over the place and the cell service here was spotty at best. No one back home knew what happened in the

197

past 24 hours. I knew that someone would send us help, but with the military still being rebuilt, Eddie and I wanted to avoid that as much as possible. "Tell us about this sworm," Eddie asked.

"It's one of the many giant, highly territorial predators we have on Komondon. It can sense movement above ground and will ambush its prey from underground. The highly toxic venom is injected into the bloodstream through biting their victims." Santa turned and looked at me. "As you experienced, Your Majesty, sworms don't immediately eat their food. They will bring it to their underground burrow and swallow it whole. Once inside their body, a needle-like appendage will pierce the prey's body and liquefy the insides. The outside of the prey becomes mummified just before the sworm returns back to the surface and spits out it." The alien paused in his matter-of-fact narration. "In fact, I believe that you and the king are among a very small handful of people who have survived a sworm attack."

Eddie and I shared the same surprised look. Overlooking the fact that Santa had just given us a very vivid description of the sworm's eating habits as if he was reading it straight from an encyclopedia article, we were unsure if our survival was supposed to be a compliment or not. "Thanks, I think?" I replied. "Is a sworm attack a regular thing on your planet?

Doris shook her head. "They rarely attack people. It's mostly livestock and other large animals. Many of our scientists would foolishly try to take an egg from one of their nests in an attempt to train it, but some of them would just observe them from a distance."

"I'm surprised it hasn't attacked the gnomes in the candy cane gumdrop forest," Eli remarked.

I instantly remembered hearing a bell ringing four times in rapid succession right before the creature broke through the frozen ground and attacked me. "Does this creature respond to bells?"

"Yes," replied Santa, "they can be trained to respond to bell ringing, but it has to be a certain kind of bell made from a metal only found on Komodon."

"That's what I heard right before I was attacked," I explained. Something clicked in my mind as a plan began to form in my mind. "Let's look at the sworm as an invasive species," I said.

"Which it is," Eli remarked dryly.

"I've got a plan. We find and confiscate the bell. Then we lure the sworm out of its hiding place and kill it."

"With what, babe?" Eddie asked. "My spells and war scythe couldn't even damage it!"

"It does have a small soft spot on the top of its head," Santa said. "One well-aimed strike could pierce the brain and kill it."

"Once the creature breaks through the ground, it'll be too fast for anyone to stop it," Eli said.

Another brilliant idea came to me. "Not unless we immobilize it first." Everyone looked at me with curiosity, especially Eddie who waited patiently to see what crazy, half-baked plan I was pulling out of my butt. "Eli, you mentioned that the sworm hasn't gone near the gumdrop forest. Maybe the gumdrops are some sort of repellant for it."

"What are you getting at, Your Majesty?" Doris asked.

"We toss a huge wad of gumdrops into the sworm's mouth and give someone enough time to run up its back and stab it." Eddie shook his head, but his face lit up. "Tossing something a huge wad of gumdrops might not work, but a potato bazooka will. Given the right materials, I can build one within an hour.”

“Eli and I can help you gather the materials, Sire,” Santa said.

“Since I came up with this plan, I’ll steal the bell and get the gumdrops,” I volunteered.

“Not without me showing you the way to the gumdrop forest, Your Majesty,” Doris said.

Chapter 11:
Twas the Fight Before Christmas

By the time Doris and I arrived at the toy factory, it had stopped snowing. The town was bathed in complete darkness, A few lights dotted the windows here and there. "I bet it's gorgeous here when the Christmas lights are on," I said.

The alien woman nodded."Yes, it is, and once we stop the sworm, Damien and Claude will face justice for their crimes against the people of Ho Hoboken."

"Good," I said. I was curious to see how justice was served in a place that celebrated the most joyous holiday in the world. Maybe they would be thrown in the same cell that Eddie and I were in earlier. But first, we needed to snag the bell. I looked around the building for a better way in than the back door. "Doris, is there any access on the roof?"

"Yes, there is a door that has a staircase behind Nick's office, but the roof door hasn't been used in several years. It might be too frozen to open."

"I'll see what I can do," I said as I started to scale the side of the factory like a spider. Once I reached the roof, I carefully slid my feet across to the door. Even though it was iced over, I managed to pry it open and quietly made my way down the concrete staircase. I listened for signs of people in the factory building but heard nothing.

Cautiously entering Santa's office, I was surprised at how low-key the room was decorated. The thin silver and gold striped wallpaper was the only thing Christmas-related in the room. A simple leather swivel chair sat behind a cedar executive desk. The papers and pens cluttering the desk barely left any room for the desktop computer and keyboard. I did a quick search but found nothing. I left the office and was about to search for another room when I heard someone scream at me

Claude stared at me in shock before he broke into a run towards me. "You're supposed to be dead!"

I turned and raced back up to the roof and was about to

close the door when Claude body-slammed it back open. I fell back and skidded almost off the roof, but scrambled to my feet. I was tempted to draw Knowledge from her sheath, but I wasn't trained for winter combat.

Bad Santa's helper was no longer a cervitaur. He was now the form of a short, horned lizard wearing the same tacky outfit when we first met. The lizardman yelled, "Prefixor Pregixenixerixal Ziggurat!" as he pulled out a bell from his coat pocket to summon the sworm. Big mistake.

I willed myself to transform into a black panther. I let out a warning roar. I crouched low and leaped forward with my front paws in front of me. Within moments, I had my jaws clamped around Claude's arm. With a sudden jerk of my head, I unintentionally tore his arm off. The bell dropped to the ground with a loud clang coupled with the lizard screaming in agony. He tried to grab his loose limb that was still clutching the sworm summoner, but I stomped on the wrist and grabbed the bell with my teeth. Claude apparently could feel any pain coming from his detached arm because he let loose another painful howl. I gave the wrist another good stomp before taking a running leap off the roof.

On my way down, I turned back into a vampire and transferred the bell from my mouth to my hands. I landed on the snowy ground in a crouch. "Got it," I told Doris.

She smiled. "Good. Now onto the Trusdale Gumdrop Forest."

The journey to the gumdrop forest wasn't too cold or long as we trudged through the snowy woods. "When we get there, we send a gnome back to Peregrin to let your family know that you and the king are all right," Mrs. Claus said.

"That would be great," I said with a smile. "Thank you." My family probably didn't know about what had happened in the past 24 hours aside from what we had told Gunther and Dusty. It would be wise to let them know what hair-brained scheme Eddie and I would be executing.

"Here we are," Doris said rather proudly the moment we entered a small clearing. "Welcome to the Trusdale Gumdrop Forest!"

Trusdale Forest was not exactly what you would call a

forest. Five large trees with connecting branches were growing in a circle in the middle of the otherwise treeless clearing. Hanging from the candy cane branches were gumdrops in varied colors the size of apples. The rainbow teardrop-shaped leaves looked like sugar-dipped fruit roll-ups.

I did a quick calculation based on my knowledge of potato guns and Eddie's creative ingenuity and quickly realized that 20 gumdrops should be more than sufficient for getting rid of the sworm. I reached for my gumdrop when I realized that I had nothing to store the gumdrops in. "Do you have a bag or something I can put these in?" I asked.

"No, I don't," Doris replied. "Can you put them in your coat pocket?"

"I don't think 20 gumdrops can fit in either one of them."

"How big is the king's potato gun going to be?"

I shrugged. "Better safe than sorry."

"We can ask Dolly and Odette Enfield, the leaders of the gnomes, but they are in hiding. I haven't seen any of them since Damien and Claude appeared."

A rustle in the leaves above us caught my attention. I

looked up to see a familiar figure running along a branch overhead. "Hey, Phoebe!" I said as I waved to the pink-and-blue-haired gnome. "Glad to see you're okay"

She skidded to a stop and looked down at me with a grin. "Thanks," she said. "I wouldn't put purple gumdrops in a potato gun. They're the stickiest and might jam the barrel."

"You certainly know a lot about potato guns."

"Yeah, my mom told me about this one kid who wanted a potato machine gun from Santa, and she saw some of the toy maker elves test it out with gumdrops."

"Did that kid happen to be my husband?"

The gnome shook her head as she jumped off the branch and landed on my shoulder. She took one look at Doris standing next to me as her eyes widened in shock. "Mrs. Claus?" She exclaimed a little too close to my ear. "I thought you were dead?"

"It's a long story, but the real Nick and I are definitely alive. We've just been in hiding."

A little door on a tree trunk opened, and two tiny women, one with blue and white striped hair and the other with pink and white striped hair, stepped onto a branch near my shoulder.

"Phoebe Enfield, what have your mother and I told you about leaving the safety of the tree?" The pink-and-white-haired woman crossed her arms over her simple gray cashmere sweater as she stared down the teenager.

"Mum!" Phoebe said with a roll of her eyes. "I'm still near the tree."

"Do not roll your eyes at your mother, young lady," said the other woman as she placed her hands on her hips.

"Yes, Mom," Phoebe replied.

The blue-haired gnome gasped the moment she saw me. "Odette," she said as she nudged her wife in the side, "it's the queen." Both gnomes bowed in my direction. "Dolly and Odette Enfield at your service. Please forgive our daughter's recklessness."

"No worries," I assured them. "I was a teenager once. I have a–." I stopped mid-sentence as my vampiric hearing picked up the distant sound of something flying overhead.

A large saucer-like shape appeared suddenly in the cloudy skies. The entire object was completely black except for a circle of blinding lights around its center. "He's here!" Doris said as her eyes widened in shock.

"Who?" I asked her.

"Ziggurat, the leader of the Komodian army! I'd recognize his ship anywhere."

A small door underside of the ship opened, and a larger version of the disgusting eyeball cameras that were spying on Eddie and me earlier. The last we needed was to give away our position. An idea came to me. The only thing I needed was to make sure my aim was good.

"Take cover!" I ordered everyone as I set Phoebe back with her mothers. I quickly grabbed the largest purple gumdrop I could reach and chucked the sticky candy toward the center of the camera. A loud satisfying splat echoed throughout the meadow as the gumdrop hit the drone. It wobbled back and forth in midair as the operator was probably trying to shake off the sticky substance.

Something the size of a water balloon shot out from the spaceship. "That's a pain bomb!" Doris said in a horrified voice.

I didn't know what a pain bomb was, but it didn't sound good. Going into stupidity mode, I broke off a candy cane branch about the size of a baseball bat and another large gumdrop. Tucking the branch under my chin and stuffing the gumdrop into my coat pocket, I quickly scaled to the top of one of the trees as the deadly weapon hurled towards us.

I tossed the gumdrop up in the air and swung the branch like a baseball bat with all of my vampiric strength. The candy hit the bomb with such force that it sent the weapon back toward the spaceship. Metal clanged against metal as a huge hole tore through the side of the aircraft sending it into a crashing nose dive off in the distance with a soft boom. No screams meant that no one was hurt. "Is everyone okay?" I asked the moment I had climbed back down to the ground.

Phoebe stared at me in awe. "That was awesome!" She exclaimed as she turned to her mothers. "Mom! Mum! Did you see how the queen just batted away that rocket like it was nothing?"

"I take it everyone's okay."

"Yes, everyone is safe, thanks to you," replied Odette.

"Let me get a bag for you," Phoebe told me before she ran inside her home. Moments later, the teenage gnome came back outside struggling with a soft square object about the size of an oversized wallet. "Here you go," she said between grunts as she set it on the branch by my head.

As I took the object from her, I realized the gnome had given me a reusable plastic bag. As I unfolded it, the face of Sargent Peppermint stared back at me. With the general store being the only one in Ho Hoboken, I shouldn't have been surprised. "I think I got enough," I said as I put the twentieth gumdrop into the almost overflowing bag.

Doris and the gnomes looked at me and then at the bulging bag. "Do you think you might be overdoing it with the gumdrops, Your Majesty?" Mrs. Claus asked.

"We might need extras in case the potato gun doesn't work," I said.

The alien shrugged reluctantly and turned to the gnomes. "Tell the other gnomes to stay hidden until I or Mr. Claus come to find you." The diminutive ladies and teenager nodded and hurried back to the safety of their tree home. Doris turned to me. "We should get back to our husbands because no doubt Zagurt and his men will hunt us down for destroying his ship."

Eddie was stepping out of Eli's house to greet me by the time Doris and I got back to the sasquatch's home. Without reading his mind, the huge grin on his face told me he had gone above and beyond the completion of a simple potato gun, that and the rocket launcher made of PVC piping atop his left shoulder. "Shelly, look at this beauty!" he said proudly, showing me the handmade weapon. "It can launch projectiles up to 1,000 feet. I figured if I angled it just right, I could kill the sworm by shooting something through the back of its head."

"Cool! Will the gumdrops be problematic projectiles?" I asked as I fished one out to show him.

"Maybe," he replied as he took a closer look at it. "I'm just not sure how much damage one of these will do."

"One of them can bring down an alien general's spaceship when you hit it with a candy cane branch."

Eddie looked up at me with surprise. "How can you possibly know that?"

"Well, did you guys hear a loud crash about ten minutes ago?"

"Yes, then we saw something plummet towards—That was you?"

"I had to do something when they shot a pain bomb at Doris, the gnomes, and me."

"Why would they shoot at you?"

"I may or may not have taken out one of their camera drones when I threw a gumdrop at it." I watched as my husband stared at me in admiration. "Hey, I got the jingle bell and the gumdrops."

"And a very angry alien general," Doris said. "Your wife was amazing, sire."

"I know she is," Eddie replied with a grin. "I'm used to hearing about stuff like this. This doesn't phase me at all."

Nick and Eli emerged from the cabin and looked at me with a mixture of shock and horror on their faces. "The pain bomb will only incapacitate Ziggurat and his crew for an hour," Nick explained. "It's designed to stun, not kill."

Eddie and I looked at each other and then at the aliens and sasquatch. "That should give us plenty of time to take care of the sworm." He took the bell from me. "All right, who knows how to use this thing?"

About ten minutes later, we were all in our positions. Eddie had the potato cannon sitting on his shoulder ready to fire. Nick stood next to him ready with the first gumdrop in hand. Eli stood by with his shotgun at hand as a backup. Doris stood next to her husband ready to ring the bell.

I, on the other hand, was the furthest one away. Doris had instructed me to feel the vibrations beneath my feet so I could calculate where the sworm would break through the ground and I could make sure I wasn't in its path. My job was simple in my head: If Eddie couldn't kill it with just the potato gun, I planned to race up its back and do the deed by jamming my sword into its head. If the potato gun did its job, then I wouldn't have to do anything. I hoped for the latter as I had done enough heroics for one day.

The ringing of the jingle bell echoed through the woods, and we all waited for the creature to appear. A rustle in the bushes behind the rest of the group startled all of us. But it wasn't the sworm. Instead Claude in his reptilian form, rushed

Nick and knocked him to the ground with one sweep of his powerful tail. Because the arm I had torn off earlier was still regenerating, he clumsily pulled out a weird-looking red gun with his good arm and aimed it at Nick. "I have caught the traitor!" he gloated.

Fortunately, he didn't have time to fire it because Eddie swung the barrel of the potato gun at him. It made contact with the fake cervitaur's head with a thud, and the alien henchman crumpled to the ground. My husband took one look at Claude's noticeably shorter arm and the teeth marks. He looked at me and gave me a thumbs up, knowing full well who had torn off the arm.

A loud bang echoed through the woods, and I saw Eli rush over and shove Doris to the ground. He aimed a massive shotgun and aimed it in the direction where the noise came from. Two more reptilians emerged from the brush. One of them was the same sinister monitor lizard in desert fatigues that I had seen in my dream the other night. The other one, a frilled lizard wearing that tasteless sweater about Mrs Claus, was right behind him. Finally, we met General Ziggurat and Damien.

Damien ran towards my husband, his neck frill flared out

like an inverted umbrella. That was a dumb move on fake Santa's part because Eddie picked up one of the gumdrops and loaded it into the potato gun. He quietly said, "Nebulae!" releasing his trademark fireball spell and activating the ignition switch as he lifted the bazooka on his shoulder. A flaming ball of purple gumdrop goo shot out from the cannon and hit the reptilian alien in the chest. Damenin flew backward into a nearby tree. The impact knocked the reptilian out like one bad bulb on a string of Christmas lights.

General Zagurt seemed completely unfazed by his bounty hunter's predicament as he continued towards Nick who had just gotten to his feet. "At last, I have found the traitor, Nicholas." He glanced over at the motionless pile of Damenian. "Unlike that useless bounty hunter." He grabbed Nick by the collar of his shirt and lifted him high in the air. He unholstered a gun similar to the one Claude had and aimed it at Santa's head.

"Nick!" shouted Doris as something red and white flew towards her husband.

Nick caught her candy cane dagger with a free hand, and, without hesitation, stabbed the dictator in the throat. Blood sprayed out, turning the white snow to a crimson red. The toymaker saw his chance to break free as the general released his grip. He stabbed Ziggurat in the throat a second time. His attacker staggered back in horror as he clutched his throat in a failed attempt to stop the blood flow. Within moments the Komodian despot collapsed to the ground as his life drained from him.

Eddie and I stared in absolute shock at Nick and the bloodied knife still in his hands. We had just witnessed Santa Claus violently kill the dictator of his planet. I was literally shaken out of my state of shock as I felt the ground beneath my feet move violently. Then just like that iconic scene from Alien, the sworm burst up from the ground, scattering snow and dirt everywhere.

The potato bazooka flew out of of my husband's hands as the impact from the sworm's breech knocked him backward. The creature lunged at him, but he managed to scramble away from its sharp teeth. He grabbed the fallen weapon and began to reload it.

I knew he wouldn't make it if I didn't do something.

Pushing aside my fears of the alien creature, I began to run towards the sworm's back. In one semi-poorly executed leap, I landed on the beast's spine without much stumbling and started to run to my target: the top of the creature's head. The sworm sensed my presence and thrashed its body around in a failed attempt to throw me off. It might have worked when I was a human, but it was no match for my vampiric speed as I reached the top in a few seconds.

I took my sword with both hands and drove the blade into the top of the sworm's head with all my strength. Yellow, gloopy blood spurted out from the fatal blow, and I closed my eyes to avoid the splattering. I had enough of its bodily fluids in me, thank you very much.

A large purple object was hurled through the air and slammed into the creature's open mouth. The impact nearly sent me tumbling off the beast's head, but I was still holding onto Knowledge by her hilt. With all the noise, I barely heard my husband shout a horrified "Oh, crap!"

"Don't break the blade. Don't break the blade," I muttered to myself as the sworm thrashed about its final death throes. A few seconds later, the sworm fell to the ground with a tremendous thud. I finally released my grip on Knowledge and rolled off the sworm.

Eddie ran over to me. "Are you okay?" he asked as he reached down to help me up. "I'm so sorry. I didn't realize that you were up on top of the sworm until after I fired the potato gun."

"No worries," I replied, taking his outstretched hand to pull me on my feet. "I'm fine," I replied. "And the sworm is dead."

Eddie and I nervously glanced at the creature's body. "It's definitely dead, right?" I asked. I just hoped the beast didn't suddenly resurrect itself and try to take revenge on my husband and myself.

My husband cautiously poked the alien creature with the end of his war scythe. He readied himself to dive in front of me. When nothing happened, he quickly extracted my sword from the dead creature's head. He wiped the goopy yellow blood from the blade in a pile of snow and handed it back to me.

"And you all stopped the bad guys," I added as I looked over at the motionless bodies of Zagurat, Damien, and Claude.

"What are you going to do with these guys?"

"Eli, Doris, and I will handle everything," Nick said in a tone that told Eddie and me not to question their motives any further. "First things, first, we need to get Your Majesties home."

A thin layer of snow blanketed the town of Peregrin on Christmas morning. Eddie and I sat on our living room couch sipping our peppermint mocha coffee and watched Alonzo chasing after a red, sparkling pom-pom that I had tossed across the room. The catnip dragon went into an uncontrolled skid across the hardwood floor and did a couple of somersaults before coming to a full stop. He scrambled back on his feet, picked up the toy between his teeth, and trotted back to the couch. He dropped it at our feet and looked up at us in anticipation of another toss. Eddie picked up the pompom and threw it across the room and Alonzo darted after it.

"Now this is the type of Christmas I want," I said as I took a sip of my coffee. "No alien worm-like creatures or fake Santas and their henchmen trying to kill us. Just spending time with family."

"Unfortunately, we can't tell anyone the truth about what happened," my husband said.

"I still can't believe we both had to sign a NDA," I said.

"I can see why. Keeping the truth about Santa might endanger Ho Hoboken even further. He did say that every resident of Ho Hoboken had to sign one as well."

I nodded, understanding. "What I want to know is what happened to Ziggurat, Damien, and Claude?" I felt a sharp nip on my leg. I looked down at Alonzo who stared up at me as if we were neglecting him. "Don't bite me, you turd muffin!" I scolded the catnip dragon.

He promptly disregarded my scolding and jumped up onto my lap. I raised my coffee mug high enough to avoid damage. Alonzo stared at me for a few seconds before giving me an affectionate headbutt.

"It seemed pretty clear Ho Hoboken has its form of justice," Eddie replied as he scratched Alonzo under the chin.

"And it's best not to question it either," I added. A small white envelope tucked away in the branches of our plastic, pre-lit Christmas tree (Don't judge) caught my attention. I got up, much to Alzono's protesting meow, and retrieved it. I expected it to be a present from Eddie but was surprised to see it was addressed to both of us in bold red lettering as if someone had used a quill pen.

"Do you know where this came from?"

My husband shook his head as he got up to join me. "Nope." He cautiously inspected the envelope to determine if it was safe to open. He opened and pulled out a Christmas card with a picture of a snow-covered town at night. The silhouette of Santa riding his sleigh pulled by eight, tiny reindeer was illuminated by the bright moon centered above the town's rooftops. Eddie opened the card and we both read the note:

"I normally don't give adults personalized presents, but because Your Majesties saved Christmas I made an exception. As a gift of Ho Hoboken's deepest appreciation, please enjoy your Christmas present that I left in the garage in your courtyard. I think I got everything correct.

Sincerely, Nick and Doris Claus

Eddie and I looked at each other, puzzled. We both knew our next move. Without saying a word, we hurriedly put on our winter coats and boots and took the elevator to the main floor of the empty castle. "What do you think he gave us?" I asked as we ran out of the stand-alone garage in the large courtyard.

"A spaceship?" Eddie suggested hopefully as he unlocked the door. Once inside, he turned on the light, and we both gasped at a perfect replica of the Eggbeater. My husband ran to the pilot's door and swung it open. "It's even better than the original!" he said as he gazed in awe at the cockpit. "There's even a stealth mode feature! I can't believe the Stocking Stuffer replicated just from my blueprints!"

I opened the passenger door, and to my delight, there was a replacement $50 ugly sweater hoodie. I threw it on and was immediately captivated by its warmth. "I love it!"

Eddie looked at me like a kid in a toy store. "Want to take this baby for a Christmas spin?" He asked me as I climbed into the co-pilot's seat.

"Oh, yeah!" I said. Once we were all ready for takeoff and with a nod from my husband, I touched the remote control, and the garage roof opened up with more than enough clearance for

us. As we lifted off, I thought I could hear the ringing of distant

sleigh bells through the cacophony of the spinning propellers.

COMING SOON!

Treasure of the Undead

My Life Among the Undead:
Book 12

Batten down the hatches and hoist the sails for a swashbuckling thrill ride with the royal vampires of Peregrin, Queen Shelly and King Eddie Van Helsing, along with their daring advisors, Gunther Hornicus and Dusty Williams. Just when they thought they had seen it all, a mysterious portrait reveals the human form of their dear friend and vampire airship captain, Cassius. But no time for chit-chat, because they are being pursued by ruthless pirates, treasure hunters, and a cryptic map that leads them on a perilous mission to discover the truth about Cassius. Every step is a test of their courage and ingenuity, as they dodge danger around every corner. Will they solve the mystery before it's too late? Get ready for an epic adventure that will have you on the edge of your seat!

ABOUT THE AUTHOR

Camara M. Bragdon lives in sunny southwest Florida with her cat, Mistoffelees. When she is not writing, she brings joy and learning as a children's and teen librarian, taking pictures and telling terrible puns. This is the eleventh book in her vampire series, *My Life Among the Undead*. Visit her website at www.camarambragdonauthor.com